Surprise Love in Summit County

SUMMIT COUNTY SERIES BOOK 8

KATHERINE KARROL

Cover Design by Ideal Book Covers

Background photo by Katherine Karrol

This book is dedicated to everyone who has taken the chance to let love in.

The Summit County Series

The Summit County Series is a group of standalone books that can be read individually, but those who read all of them in order will get a little extra something out of them as they see the characters and stories they've read about previously continue and will get glimpses of characters that may be featured in future books. The series is set in a small county in northern Michigan where everyone knows everyone else, so the same characters and places make cameos and sometimes show up in significant roles in multiple books.

This series is near and dear to the author's heart because her favorite place in the world looks an awful lot like Summit County. She is certain that the people who know her and/or live in the area that inspired Summit County will think characters and situations are based on them or their neighbors (or even on her), and she assures them that they are not. The characters and stories are merely figments of her overly active imagination. Well, except for Jesus. He's totally real.

Chapter 1

IT WASN'T QUITE RIGHT. Cynthia Huntley scanned the living room once more, looking for the perfect spot. Putting the *Welcome Home* sign on the mantle seemed anti-climactic, nowhere near the hero's welcome Zachary deserved. She walked outside one more time, certain that she could find a better place for it.

Standing in the middle of the sidewalk with her hands on her hips, she stared at her front porch and visualized where it would catch Zachary's eye without being too flashy. She tilted her head and squinted in concentration as she pictured it hanging over the steps.

"Maybe it needs balloons—no, scratch that. Balloon pops can trigger PTSD reactions." She added streamers to her mental shopping list instead.

Roscoe's wagging tail and quick descent from the front porch, along with the familiar sound of heavy footsteps behind her, let her know that Wyatt had crossed the street and joined her on the lawn. His breath tickled her ear as he whispered, "What are we looking at?"

"The *Welcome Home* sign."

"Looks great."

She elbowed him in the ribs. "Very funny."

He doubled over in one of his standard attempts at hilarity. "Well, it's going to look great when you put it up. I'm just pre-complimenting you on yet another job well done."

"You don't have to kiss up to me, Wyatt. Your dinner is almost ready and I just put the chicken and corn on the grill."

He rubbed his stomach. "Good, I'm starving. Do I have time for my upper-body workout before we eat?"

"Definitely." As she led him into the house and into Zachary's room, she noticed the box he was carrying. "Hey, is that a gift for me?"

"Actually, it sort of is. I got some noise-canceling headphones for Zack. I know he said no gifts at his party, but I thought he might accept one if it was something that would help him."

He was so thoughtful. Zachary would love them. "That's a great gift. They'll come in handy when people start in with Labor Day fireworks in a couple of weeks."

He winked. "And when he wants to listen to Metalopia."

"Yes!" She threw her arms around him. "Wyatt, you did give me a gift!"

"Told you." He set the box on Zachary's dresser and assessed the fabric bolts that were neatly stacked on the bed.

"As much as I'm going to miss having the extra storage space, I can't wait to have Zachary home."

His smile met hers. "I know, and he'll appreciate not having all these girly fabrics in here when he gets home tomorrow." He picked up several of the bolts of fabric and headed to her workroom. "This time will be a whole different homecoming than when he came back from Walter Reed. You finally get to throw a party."

"I'm so excited." She stopped herself from clapping her hands in glee as she followed him. "Thank you again for my new shelves. They're perfect for the fabric."

"You're very welcome. Bottom shelf?"

She chuckled. "It's scary how well you know my organization system. I'm going to go make the salad while you finish up. Don't pull any muscles—we're going to need them for cornhole at the party."

He saluted her as he strode toward Zachary's room for another armful. "What's with all this extra fabric, anyway?"

She answered back as she walked to the kitchen. "Two party dresses, a bridal veil, Fall Festival projects, and a few fabrics that were on sale and begging me to make something out of them. I finished the rest of the alteration orders I had this afternoon."

"Yeah, I've noticed your lights on later than usual."

"I've been too excited to sleep the last couple of days, so I decided to work instead."

He entered the kitchen and pulled the tongs out of the drawer. "Excited or nervous?"

"A little of both, I suppose." Her hands fell still over the salad. "He's sounded so good on the phone since he's been at the Veteran's Ranch, but I'm afraid to get my hopes up. PTSD doesn't just go away."

"True, but he's sounded great the last few times I've talked to him, and they wouldn't discharge him if he wasn't ready. Four months is long enough for them to know, right?"

She sure hoped so. Either way, God had Zachary under His wing. "Right. I'm glad he'll be here for a few days before the party so I can see for myself how he's doing. I've already told everyone that if he's struggling, I'm canceling it."

"Good call. I don't think you'll need to though." He headed out the back door to retrieve the chicken and corn from the grill.

By the time Wyatt returned, Cynthia was seated at the table. When he sat and took her hand before saying grace, she was overwhelmed with thankfulness for his presence in her life. "Thank you for everything, Wyatt."

"It was only five minutes of lifting things, Cyn."

Her eyes started to sting. "You know what I mean. That day . . ."

"You've already thanked me for that, and I've already told you there were no thanks needed." His large hand surrounded hers. "I told you I would be here if you and Zack needed me. I'm just sorry you did."

She nodded. "And now he's better, and I get to throw the party I thought might never happen. Did I mention you're in charge of the grill?"

"Cynthia Marie, I'm offended that there would be a question of whether or not I'm manning the grill. Of course I'm in charge of it."

"Okay, Chef. Settle down." She chuckled. "Say grace for us before the food gets cold."

Chapter 2

SOMETIMES WYATT HENRY HATED his job. He exhaled slowly and spoke in a measured tone. "Put the gun down, Gus."

"You first."

"You know that's not how it works." Wyatt studied Gus's hand in his peripheral vision while keeping his eyes trained on his face. "You know I don't want to hurt you."

"If I put mine down, you're just gonna pull out your stupid cuffs." He practically teetered as the words slurred out of his mouth. "I'm not goin' to jail again. I'm not!"

"I'd rather take you to jail than the hospital, Gus—or worse yet, the morgue. Work with me here."

Gus finally looked at him. His eyes were wild with fear.

Wyatt calmly held his gaze. "I know you're scared, Gus." He tilted his head in the direction of Gus's long-suffering girlfriend, shielding herself behind the tattered couch. "So is Maggie."

Maggie spoke through her tears. "Please, Gus. Do what he says. I'll come visit you as soon as they let me." She stretched her hand toward him, pleading.

Again.

Wyatt had to keep his thoughts and focus centered on the teetering man and not the woman who returned to him time after time despite years of drunkenness and threats. This time she wasn't even making a pretense of leaving.

One would think that knowing every law enforcement officer and bail bondsman in the area by name would influence her decisions. Of course, one would think that staring into the barrel of a revolver—again—would too. It was as if she had just accepted nights like this as part of her relationship. Or that she was completely broken.

Wyatt's arm was getting tired, and he hoped Gus's was too. "Gus . . . let's end this peacefully. Put the gun down. Maybe this can be the time that things change for you two." He had been called to the run-down farmhouse too many times to believe a word of that, but he said what he needed to in these situations and hoped that someday change really would happen.

"Please, Gus. I'm sorry, baby." Maggie's voice was barely a squeak.

Gus stared at her with an ever-shifting expression. The fear and anger seemed to be dissipating, and Wyatt prayed that reason would take over—not that reasoning was Gus's strong suit.

After a moment Gus lowered the gun and sighed. "That's all I wanted to hear."

Wyatt bit the inside of his cheek to keep his words to himself and hide his irritation at the man's sense of entitlement and complete lack of self-awareness. He had very little patience for men who took out their anger and insecurities on women, especially ones he had to drag away on a regular basis.

Don't react. Get the job done and get her to safety.

"Good job, Gus. Set the gun on the floor and push it to Officer Brody."

"I know." He rolled his eyes and spat the words. "This is not my first rodeo."

No kidding. I'm getting sick of the bull at this particular one.

Gus finally acquiesced, setting the gun on the worn wood floor and sliding it toward Brody with his foot, all the while glaring at

Wyatt. As Brody cuffed him and walked him out to the car, Wyatt had to block the door to stop Maggie from running after them.

"You know you can't do that, Maggie."

"Can't I just say goodbye?" She tried to lean around Wyatt's large frame.

"You can talk to him tomorrow. Right now you need to let us do our job."

"But he didn't mean it."

"Maggie, look at me." The desperate woman's tears jerked at his heart. "Whether he meant it or not, and whether he's sorry tomorrow or not, he could have killed you. It's my job to try to prevent that from happening."

She stood sobbing as Wyatt reached into his pocket and pulled out the card with the domestic violence hotline number on it and handed it to her. Again.

It was a waste of time and paper giving it to her, but he needed to do something. She probably had the number memorized by now, or at least on speed dial.

"I wish I could do more for you, Maggie." He reached over to the tissue box and handed one to her. "I wish you would let me."

With her, he meant every word. Unfortunately, the only way he could think of to help her was to kidnap her and get her out of the situation long enough to wake up. Last he heard, that was still illegal. "There are people who can help you. The shelter is there, waiting, but it's up to you now. Call them . . . please, Maggie."

She nodded, looking at the floor. "I will. Thank you, Officer Henry."

You'll call, but you won't give the shelter another thought. He wished he had the power to make people stop lying to themselves, but that was far above his pay grade.

As he walked the gravel path to the car, he asked God to give her courage and strength to get out. The love he once had for his job was waning, and situations like the one he'd spent the last hour in wore him out. He needed to schedule a day to get out on Lake

Michigan, where the only weapons he needed were lures, rods, and nets, and he needed to do it soon.

He had learned as an MP in the Marines more than twenty years ago that too many domestic calls could wear a person down and that regular R and R was a necessity of the job. It was a toss-up which was worse, a civilian inadequately trained in firearm safety who made a hobby of getting drunk and threatening his girlfriend, or a highly-trained Marine who snapped after too many deployments. Either way, his least favorite call was one that could end with someone getting hurt.

Checking his watch, he was pleasantly surprised that his shift was already over. *Time flies when you're reasoning with armed drunks.*

Brody would take care of processing Gus and it would take Wyatt no time to do the report, so his day was almost over. Too bad there was no copy-and-paste for that. All that ever changed on a domestic disturbance call to Gus's place was the date and time. In a small town like Hideaway, even the names of the arresting officers were usually the same.

His stomach growled and reminded him of the enchiladas Cynthia had promised him. He had been thinking about them since she texted a picture of them earlier, and he was more than ready to indulge. Between her cooking and her company, his day would be getting better soon.

Chapter 3

CYNTHIA WAS SITTING ON her front porch listening to an audiobook and enjoying the warm August breeze when Wyatt pulled into his driveway across the street. She breathed the usual sigh of relief and prayer of thanks as she waved. *Thank You, Lord, for bringing him back in one piece.*

Wyatt was her best friend, and it was the least she could do to pray for his safety until he arrived home from work. The large porch on her Craftsman house was a perfect prayer room, and she sat out there as often as the northern Michigan weather allowed. He usually went into his house to shower and change out of his uniform before coming over, so when he walked straight to her porch from his truck, she knew it must have been a rough shift.

His footsteps were heavy as he made his way up the stairs. "I need a drink."

She stood and walked toward the door that led into the house. "The usual?"

"I can get it."

"You look whipped. Have a seat, and I'll be right back."

She hurried into the kitchen, put the enchiladas she'd set aside for him earlier into the toaster oven, and pulled out the biggest glass in the cupboard. She smiled as she filled a small bowl with

Wyatt's favorite sauce. Now that Zachary was back home, he had made a big batch of the "recipe" he had learned from one of his platoon buddies. It was just two different store-bought jars combined, but Wyatt and Zachary thought it was the greatest invention since enchiladas themselves.

When she returned to the porch, he had a far-away look in his eyes. His gaze landed well past the trees that formed a canopy over the street.

She held out the glass to him. "Leftovers are heating up, and I made you a double. Even an extra lemon twist, on the house."

His tired smile showed his appreciation as he took the glass. "You sure know how to greet a guy after a long day. A double of the best homemade lemonade in town is just what the doctor ordered."

"Good. Rough one?"

"Yeah." He rubbed his face with his hand and ran it through his short hair. "Ended with a domestic out on Laske Road."

"Laske Road, huh? Should I be expecting a call from Maggie when I take my shift on the hotline this week?"

He shrugged and frowned, his blue eyes looking darker in the evening light. "Hard telling. I reminded her about the shelter again. I wish she would get out of there. The last time was only a few weeks ago."

"Well, I'll be praying that we hear from her and that she'll give the shelter a try this time."

Sadness and frustration shone in his eyes when he looked at her. "How do you do it? How do you take those calls from the same women over and over?"

She sipped her own lemonade and pictured the women and children at the shelter. "I keep my focus on what I can do. I can't make them leave, but I can listen and offer them information about their options. And I can donate homemade snacks and alterations to the families at the shelter. It's not much, but it's something." The toaster oven dinged, signaling that the enchiladas were ready, and she opened the front door. "I also never forget that I was in their shoes once. It took me a long time to leave too."

Chapter 4

A WEEK LATER, WYATT was in Cynthia's back yard for Zack's long-awaited welcome home party. He beat his chest like a gorilla as he pranced around in a circle. "I am the king of cornhole!"

"Hey, what about your partner?" Cynthia, hands on her hips, did her best to look offended.

"And this is my queen!" He gestured toward her and took a deep bow.

She snickered and took on a haughty pose, tossing her blonde hair. "I prefer empress."

"My empress!"

When he reached out to raise her hand in victory, they danced around together.

Zack laughed even as he groaned. "You two are definitely the king and queen—excuse me, *empress* of obnoxious winners."

He seemed to be doing well in the few days since he had returned from the sixteen-week program for veterans with PTSD and prosthetics. He was much closer now to the carefree guy he'd been before losing a leg and much of his innocence at war than when he'd left for the program a few months back.

"Don't worry, Zack. We'll give your team the prize for most gracious lose—uh, *non-winners*."

Zack and his teammate and best friend, Laci Ryan, both stuck their tongues out at Wyatt before Zack spoke for both of them. "Yeah, whatever. We want a rematch."

Cynthia grinned sarcastically and stuck her hands up in an "oh well" pose. "Sorry, but I've got to go get the food out and Wyatt has to man the grill. We'll beat you again after we eat though, if you'd like." She high-fived Wyatt and strutted toward the house while Zack and Laci shook off their loss and invited Cynthia's brother, Mitch, and his girlfriend, Bella, to a game.

Wyatt snickered at the pair. "You go ahead and practice on them. It will make the victory sweeter if you make it more of a challenge for us next time."

Zack and Laci rolled their eyes at each other, nodded, and threw their bean bags at Wyatt, hitting their target more than once. They giggled like children at their success.

"Hey, you're assaulting a police officer!" Wyatt hurled the bags back in their direction, mostly hitting Zack after he stepped in front of Laci.

When Wyatt entered the kitchen a moment later, he found Cynthia looking out the kitchen window with a smile on her face and tears brimming in her eyes.

She turned to him when he walked through the door. "Don't mind me. I didn't know if I was ever going to get to throw anything resembling a welcome home party for him." Her tears refused to be restrained any longer and clouded her hazel eyes. "I'm so happy he's here and getting closer to being himself."

When Wyatt took her into his embrace, she wrapped her arms around his waist and burrowed her face into his chest. They had shared many such hugs in the year since Zack had returned home from the front lines, but most of the tears she had shed were from grief and fear, not joy and relief. It was a welcome change.

She backed away and wiped her eyes with the back of her hand. "Sorry, I just had a moment."

"I know. You're entitled to all the moments you need." Not seeing any tissues when he looked around, he handed her a napkin. "It's been a rough time, and you and your brother have been the strong ones for him. You're allowed to have a little breakdown here and there now that he's out of danger."

"Thanks. With all the breakdowns you've been around for, I'm surprised you don't move away from here. Or at least show up with an apron to keep your clothes dry."

"Move away from you? And miss all the good food?" He reached out to put his hand on her shoulder and squeeze it. "This stuff is what friends are for, right? Speaking of aprons, the grill is hot and I came in for the meat. Take your time in here, and I'll take the rest of the food out."

"Have I mentioned how awesome you are lately?"

He scratched at the stubble on his chin. "I'm not sure. You should probably tell me again so I don't forget." Lifting the tray that held the meat, he captured her gaze. "Seriously, Cyn, take as long as you need."

She took a deep breath and exhaled, readying herself to join the others. "I'm good, and I'm ready to continue the party." After picking up the vegetable tray, she stopped in the doorway. "Wyatt?"

"Yeah?"

"I know I'm not supposed to thank you again, but part of the reason we're able to have this party today is because of you. You helped save Zachary's life, and I can never repay you." She hurried out the door before she saw his eyes mist.

Chapter 5

CYNTHIA WAS PULLING THE last of the dishes out of the dishwasher a few days later when Zachary walked into the kitchen in gym shorts and a faded Army t-shirt. "I can't believe that you barely have a limp now. All of your hard work in physical therapy has paid off for you."

She took in the sight of him. He still wore his brown hair cropped short, and he was as fit as he had been before the IED tore through his tank and changed his life forever. If someone only saw him from the waist up, they would think he was still on active duty.

"Yeah, this new liner helps too. I'm glad they convinced me to try one more after the other three didn't. I'm not quite where I want to be, but I'm gonna get there." He reached out to take the plates from her and took them to the cupboard. "Thanks again for the party the other day, Mom. It was really fun."

"Thank you for letting me have one. I know you don't like being the center of attention, but everyone wanted to celebrate you."

"I know. I appreciate it. I was glad for the chance to thank people in person and eye-to-eye for all the cards and prayers."

She gathered up some coffee cups and chuckled. "I'm sorry for humiliating you and Laci on the cornhole court."

"You are not." He snickered as he closed the cupboard door and reached for the cups. "I'm still convinced that you and Wyatt figured out a way to cheat, but whatever."

"Scout's honor, there was no cheating going on." She crossed her heart with her finger. "You and Laci make a good team. We barely beat you."

"Don't try to make me feel better about losing, Mom. Especially after rubbing our faces in it."

She bit her lip, trying to suppress her giggle. "Sorry."

He laughed with her. "You've really got to work on your fake sincerity." He started to leave the room, then turned back toward her, suddenly looking serious.

"Mom?"

"Yeah?"

"I'm glad you left Kirk when you did."

She inhaled sharply. *Whoa.* "Where did that come from?"

Zachary had been asking a lot of questions about her relationship with his abusive father over the past few weeks, so she shouldn't have been surprised, but she was still not accustomed to him bringing up that topic.

"Nowhere. I was just thinking that you gave me a great party the other day, but you've given me a great life too. I didn't miss anything not having a father around, and I'm glad neither of us have to deal with him anymore."

She smiled at the son she was so proud of. "I appreciate you saying that. I always worried about it, but I thought it was better for you to have an absent father than one who hurt you and taught you all the wrong things."

He walked back into the room and kissed her cheek. "I had you and Grandma and Grandpa and Mitch. I had everything I needed." As he started through the doorway, he turned back with a shrug. "And for the past ten years, I've even had Wyatt."

When he was fully out of the room, she exhaled. Her sweet little boy had grown into quite the man. *Lord, that was all You.*

Thank You for protecting him from what he could have seen and could have become. Thank You for giving him good men to learn from—and thank You for making him more like my father than his.

Chapter 6

WYATT WHISTLED TO HIMSELF in his kitchen while he filled his thermos with coffee. The tile was cool in the predawn hour, but having it freeze his bare feet was helping him wake up as much as the coffee would.

The winds that were howling when he went to bed at eleven had settled down quite a bit, so they wouldn't cause a big problem on the day's fishing expedition. Three- to four-foot waves were manageable, and the group that had chartered the boat he owned with an old friend were regulars who knew what they were doing. It was always easier taking experienced people out, but especially when the rain was still pouring down. This would be a good day for R and R indeed.

Even though investing in the boat had been a bit of an impulse buy, it had turned into a decent side job that took his mind off some of the things he had to deal with on occasion at work. If it wasn't for the boat, his friends, and his faith, his job might eat him alive. At least he got to live and work in a small town. He never would have made it in a big city.

He had always wanted to follow in his uncle's footsteps and go into law enforcement, even after the man's death in the line of duty. The reality that the job carried high stakes with it had never deterred him. It was a practical way to make a difference in the community, and he had honed a good set of diplomacy skills over his eight years in the Marines and fifteen on the mostly quiet streets of Hideaway.

He tried to move quietly and quickly in the dark as he loaded his gear into the back of his truck, but Roscoe started barking from Cynthia and Zack's front window as soon as he saw him. Wyatt and Roscoe were buddies too, so Roscoe was always quick to remind Wyatt of the tradition of giving him treats.

He muttered under his breath. "That dog barks every time a squirrel has gas." He was actually happy about that fact, because as much as it annoyed him at times, he would rather have a dog that barked too much than not enough protecting two people he considered family.

The front door opened, and Zack gave a sleepy wave as he led Roscoe down the steps to do his morning business. The rain had all but stopped by that point, but they were still getting damp. Roscoe pulled against the leash and whined as he tried to get across the street to Wyatt.

Wyatt walked toward the street and used his best stage whisper to avoid waking any other neighbors up. "Sorry, Zack. I tried to be quiet."

"I know. I decided to get him out before he wakes my mom up. You headed out fishing?"

"Yup. Got a charter group this morning. You let me know when you're ready to get back out onto the lake."

Zack looked down at his prosthetic leg. "I'm ready. This thing isn't gonna stop me." Looking up at the sky, he chuckled. "Maybe on a less ugly day though."

"You're on. If there's any extra fish today, I'll bring it over later."

"Sounds like dinner is on you." Zack smiled as he started leading the dog back to the house before he could find something else to bark at.

Wyatt was about to get into his truck when Zack turned and walked back across the street. "Wyatt, hold up."

"What's up?"

"There's something I've wanted to say since I got back home last week."

"What's on your mind?"

Zack looked down at Roscoe, who had found something to sniff under Wyatt's truck. "I just want to say thank you for what you did for me before I left."

Wyatt felt his throat tighten with emotion. "You know that no thanks are needed. I'm glad I could help." Sometimes it was difficult being a cop in a small town, and there were times when he had to be there in an official capacity for the worst moments of his friends' and neighbors' lives. The day he had to go to Zack and Cynthia's house while on duty four months ago was one of the hardest of his career. Of his life, really.

Zack rubbed the back of his neck. "I wasn't thinking about hurting myself that day, but after hearing the stories from the other guys and women at the Ranch, I know that could have changed." His voice was as full of emotion as Wyatt felt. "I'm glad you and Mitch got me to the hospital before things got worse, and I'll always be thankful for you."

When he stuck his hand out, Wyatt pulled him into a hug. "You're family to me, Zack. I wouldn't want to see anything happen to you or your mom."

"I know." Zack pulled on Roscoe's leash to get him out from under the car. "I'll bet you didn't see all this coming when you moved in here and started hiring me to do stuff for you that you could have done yourself."

Wyatt laughed. "You figured that out, huh?"

"I was young, but I wasn't stupid. I thought maybe you needed a friend, being new in town. Now I realize that you knew I did."

"You were a good kid, and I liked having you here. My dad always said the road to manhood was paved with skills, so I tried to give you some." He hoisted the cooler into the truck bed. "It helped that you already knew your way around a toolbox, thanks to helping your grandpa at the hardware store. You did good work for me, and it was worth every penny."

"It didn't hurt that my mom saw what you were doing and started sending snacks over with me when I came to 'work' for you." Zack grinned along with his air quotes.

"You know, since we're showing our cards from those days, I'm pretty sure your mom was using snacks as an excuse to check me out and make sure I was on the up and up." He smiled, remembering the subtle ways she'd asked questions. She could give a spy a run for his money. "I think it took a good six months before she really felt comfortable having you come over to my house."

"Yeah, she was a tad bit overprotective of me, wasn't she?" He chuckled as he looked down at Roscoe, as if contemplating whether or not to continue. "I remember thinking you two were gonna start dating and I was going to lose my friend. I told my mom she couldn't have you."

Wyatt laughed, probably loud enough to wake a neighbor or two. "You did? Well, I'm glad it didn't stop her from being my friend too. Or especially from sending snacks."

His friendship with Cynthia had gotten both of them through some hard times over the past ten years and had helped to hold the loneliness of being a single man and living alone at bay. Choosing a career in law enforcement over marriage and family was hard, but he felt like service was his calling, and God used Cynthia and Zack to fill in the gaps for him. Cynthia had her own reasons for remaining single, and their comfortable friendship had filled in gaps for her as well.

"Yeah, she does have a way with the snacks." His arm jerked as Roscoe pulled at the leash. "Anyway, I'm going to get Roscoe in before he starts noticing that the squirrels are already awake. I just wanted to thank you and tell you that I'm glad you moved here when you did."

"Best ten years of my life. You've come a long way from that kid, you know. You're a good man, and I'm proud to call you friend."

Zack grinned as he turned and walked toward the street. "Show me by bringing me some salmon tonight."

"You're on."

Chapter 7

Cynthia stared at the bolts of fabric in front of her, wondering how on earth she was going to get the huge project done before the Fall Festival.

She didn't have a lot of free time, so scheduling was going to be key. Her regular alteration and dressmaking business kept her plenty busy, as did the alterations she made on donated clothing so that the women and children at the shelter didn't have to look like they were wearing borrowed clothes.

If she was going to have any chance of making headway on the Festival items before dark, she needed some refreshments. Starting to feel overwhelmed and cranky, she let her snarky attitude fly to get it out of her system while she sliced an apple and poured a new glass of iced tea. "Cynthia, it would be so great if we could have matching aprons and hats for the chili cook-off this year . . . Oh, sure, we'll all help and it will be a fun group project . . . Hey, did we mention that we decided to have *all* the volunteers wear the aprons? That won't be a problem, right? . . . Oh, shoooot, I don't have time to help. I forgot and made other plans . . . You're so much better at this, being such a good professional seamstress and all. Maybe it would be easier if you just do it and we'll stay out of your way."

Muffled laughter came from the back porch, and she looked up to see Wyatt standing there listening to her diatribe.

"Are you having fake arguments in your head with the church ladies again?" He strode through the screen door and followed her as she walked back into the bedroom she used as a workspace.

"These aren't fake conversations. These actually happened. I'm just recapping them."

He sighed. "They stood you up again?"

"Again. Church ladies are the worst." She laughed as she pictured the church lady character from an old TV show sitting in the Fall Festival planning meeting.

"You know you technically are one, right?"

"Oh, I'm the worst kind. I'm the one who keeps agreeing to things and then is surprised when the others don't help. Then I gripe about them to myself while I'm doing the latest supposed group project alone."

He leaned against the doorway, filling a good part of it. "Well at least you're only griping to yourself. That is, unless your nosy neighbor is eavesdropping on you."

"I don't usually expect an audience. Good thing I don't gripe about you much."

"Much? Ha! What could you possibly have to gripe about when it comes to me?"

She rolled her eyes teasingly. "Oh, believe me, there are things."

"What things?"

Something on his pant leg caught her eye. "Your pants, for starters."

"Pardon me?" He looked down at his uniform. "These are Hideaway Police Department originals. They're the rage on all the law enforcement fashion runways."

She did a twirling motion with her finger. "Turn ninety degrees, Mr. Supermodel. Now look in that mirror at the reflection from this mirror."

"Oh, man! Where did that rip come from?" He smacked his hand to his head. "Mrs. Burgess's dog. That stupid, stupid dog."

Roscoe whimpered from his bed in the corner of the room and put his head on his outstretched paws.

"Not you, buddy. You're loud, but you're smart. You would never try to eat my pants."

"Behind the screen." Cynthia pointed to the screen that created a dressing corner in her workspace. "Give me your pants."

He snickered at her, holding his ground. "You aren't getting my pants."

She tilted her head and gave him her most stern look. "You're in uniform, Wyatt. You're obviously on your way to work. Stop arguing, get behind the screen, and give me your pants."

"Fine." He started taking off his belt as he strutted toward the screen.

"Spare me the strip tease. Hang on and I'll get a sheet to put around you." She giggled as she walked to the linen closet. The old flat sheet of her mother's with the bright, obnoxious flower pattern would be perfect.

When she returned, his pants were hanging over the screen and he sang in a high-pitched voice. "No peeking!"

"You wish!" She tossed the sheet over the screen and grabbed the pants in one smooth motion. "This will only take a sec."

When he sashayed out from behind the screen, she couldn't help but laugh. Seeing the tall, burly Marine-turned-cop in a flowered sheet was too much.

"Wyatt, you need a woman."

"Why? Because I can rock a flowered skirt?"

"Yes." *And because you're too good to be alone.*

He flexed his muscles and struck a bodybuilder pose. "You're looking at someone who is comfortable in his manhood, lady."

"I'll admit, I've never seen flowers look so manly."

"These blue ones match my eyes, no?"

"Almost."

He gestured toward the sewing machine that she was deftly using to make his torn pants look brand new. "Less gawking, more working, please. And no pictures."

"I'm almost done." She paused the machine, reached into her pocket, pulled out her phone, and took a picture. "Oops!"

"You didn't."

She cut the thread with her teeth as she batted her eyes. "Didn't what?"

"If you show anyone that picture, I'll arrest you for defamation."

Looking at the picture, she shrugged. She'd taken it so fast that his head was cut off. "You'll have to prove it's you to arrest me. This is just a torso in a flowered skirt."

He tried grabbing the phone when she turned it toward him, but she was too quick and stuck it back into her pocket. "Better luck next time. I think I just found my new home screen." She tossed his pants to him. "Now put your pants on and get out of here."

He laughed as he ducked behind the screen again. "Words you never thought you would say to me."

"I also never thought I would have a picture of you in a flowered skirt."

"You can't prove that's me. It's just a torso."

A few days later, Cynthia was sketching ideas for a vintage wedding dress she was redesigning when she got a text from Madison Rankin, a real estate agent from Lakes End. Madison had just gone on a shopping spree for new work clothes and was in need of alterations. She had been going to Cynthia's church for about a year and coming for alterations for a few months, and Cynthia had liked her from the beginning.

Wyatt's face sprang to mind and she remembered what Zachary had said about positive influences in his life. Wyatt would have made a great dad, even though he had always said that he wouldn't marry or have kids when he had a career that could put him in the line of fire. Watching what his aunt and cousins went through after his uncle's death had a big effect on him, but maybe he had softened that stance. He was only forty-three, three years older than Cynthia, and he looked and acted much younger. There was still time for him to have a family and for some lucky kids to have a great dad.

Madison seemed like a woman worthy of a man like Wyatt. She and Cynthia had met when she was new at the church and joined the women's Bible study that Cynthia led. Cynthia always enjoyed the insights she brought to the discussion and thought she was a smart and caring woman. She had never been married, and Cynthia knew that she wished for a family. She was only thirty-five or thirty-six, so several years younger than Wyatt, but in Cynthia's experience men never seemed to mind age differences as long as it was the women who were younger. The fact that she had beautiful round eyes, chestnut hair falling down her shoulders, and curves in most of the right places didn't hurt either.

She mentally pictured Wyatt's work schedule before giving Madison available appointment times. It felt good to give a potential gift to two deserving people. She had never tried matchmaking before, but maybe she had a talent for it. Wouldn't it be wonderful to find Wyatt's dream woman for him?

Chapter 8

WYATT GLANCED AT HIS watch. When Cynthia had texted him and asked if he would help her with her leaf blower, she had asked him to come at seven. It was unusual for her to specify a time, but she was busy with several alteration projects in addition to the Fall Festival one, so she was swamped. She was probably just used to giving people appointments to keep her schedule in line.

He had been waiting for the car in her driveway to leave, but when it was still there at seven-fifteen, he went over anyway. She greeted him with a broad smile when he walked in.

Suspiciously broad.

"Hi, neighbor!" What was with the overly-happy greeting?

He narrowed his eyes. "Hi . . ."

"Thanks for coming."

Thanks?

He kept his voice low, not knowing who was in the house with her. "What are you up to?"

"Nothing. I'm just finishing up with a client and must have lost track of time."

A woman he'd never seen before walked out of the sewing room.

"Wyatt, this is Madison. Madison, this is my neighbor, Wyatt."

My neighbor? Did I just move in?

"He's just here to help me out with something."

Wyatt and Cynthia were both always quick to clarify that they were just friends to others who assumed something different, but she was really laying it on thick for this woman.

He shook hands with the woman, who looked to be in her mid-thirties. "Nice to meet you. Cynthia is the best seamstress around, so you're in good hands."

"Oh, don't I know it." She had a big, friendly smile and seemed to know Cynthia, even though she was unfamiliar to him.

He tried to excuse himself and let Cynthia get back to work. "I don't want to intrude, so I'll leave you to finish up while I go take a look at the leaf blower."

"There's no rush. We were just talking, and Madison was telling me she loves to fish." Gesturing to Wyatt, Cynthia spoke to Madison. "Wyatt has a charter boat. He got a huge king salmon the other night, and it was delicious. That was probably because he grilled it to perfection though."

Why is she acting so weird? If he didn't know better, he would think she was trying to set them up.

When Madison started asking about the haul from the other night, Cynthia excused herself and walked into her bedroom. Madison didn't look like someone who would bait her own hook, let alone clean a fish, but maybe it was the curve-hugging dress and high heels that she was wearing that threw him off. She had a look that fit in far better in an executive office than on a fishing boat.

The irony struck him once again that Cynthia's alterations could flatter any woman's figure and make them look like a million dollars, but she clothed herself in baggy, long, nondescript items. It might be more accurate to say she barricaded herself in them. She did everything possible to play down her natural beauty even though she was gifted at playing up the beauty of others.

He and Madison chatted about favorite Summit County fishing spots and recipes for a few minutes until finally Cynthia returned with no explanation of where she had been.

Madison hugged Cynthia goodbye. "Thank you again, Cynthia. Everything is going to look fabulous, as always. Let me know when it will be ready, and I'll arrange to come pick it up."

"You're welcome. And thank you again for donating the clothes for the shelter. Those suits are going to go a long way toward helping someone get a job."

"Good. I'm glad to help, and I don't need a closet full of clothes that I don't wear." Madison turned to Wyatt and extended her hand. "It was nice meeting you, Wyatt. Maybe I'll see you on the big lake."

"Sounds good. Nice to meet you too."

When she closed the door behind her, Cynthia turned to him with the same suspicious smile she had greeted him with when he walked in earlier. "She's nice, huh?"

"Seems so, yeah."

"I know her from church. She's so sweet and pretty." She watched the woman get into her car and drive away. "Can you believe she's single?"

Oh, geez.

He shook his head. "Well that explains your weirdness."

"What weirdness? I'm just saying."

"Why does everyone think I need a woman so badly?"

Cynthia looked down for a moment. "Because you're a good man, and you should have a chance to share your life with someone."

He shook his head. "*Et tu*, Cynthia? You think I don't get enough offers to fix me up every Sunday from the ladies at my church?"

"Maybe we're onto something and you should try it." She tapped her finger on her chin as if conjuring up an idea. "Maybe you should come to my church this Sunday, and you can see Madison again."

Oh, brother. "Maybe I should fix your leaf blower."

She turned and sauntered back to the sewing room. "The leaf blower is fine."

Chapter 9

THE DINING ROOM TABLE was perfect for laying out fabric and patterns. Cynthia was way behind on the aprons and hats for the Fall Festival, and she was trying to create an assembly line to catch up.

"Do you need me to help, Mom?" Zachary had just gotten home from a long day working at Mitch's hardware store. He always limped more when he was tired, and judging by his gait, he was whipped.

"No, I'm good." If she was honest, she wasn't good. Her back was sore from bending over the fabric to cut it, and her eyes were tired from focusing on the lines. Zachary had done enough for the day though.

She leaned back and stretched. "I think it's time for me to call it a day. Want to sit on the porch with me?"

As if it would have his answer, he looked down at his phone screen. "Sure."

"Are you waiting for a call?"

He held the front door open for her to walk through before following her outside. "Laci and I were supposed to hang out, but I haven't heard from her."

Call it mother's intuition, but something was up. "Is everything okay?"

He paused and fidgeted with his phone. "Can I ask you a question without you assuming anything or jumping to conclusions?"

Uh-oh. Probably not. "Sure."

"When you talk to the women who call you sometimes, the ones in bad relationships . . . what do you say to them?" He looked sad as he talked, as if it were a plea for help rather than information.

It dawned on her that every time Zachary brought up her relationship with his violent father or her work with abused women lately, it was right after Laci had been mentioned.

Her heart fell. *Not sweet Laci.*

"Is something going on with Laci?"

His face flushed and he looked down at the blank screen.

"Honey?"

When he looked back up, his sad eyes were those of the little boy who saw his father hurt his mother way too many times.

"I think something is going on with her and her boyfriend, and I think her brother does too."

"Has Garrett said something to you?"

"Not outright, but he came into the hardware store the other day and asked me some questions about her boyfriend, who by the way is a total tool." Zachary's brow was furrowed. "I don't know. Garrett sees the same stuff in her that I see, and he's sure that it's because of Ronnie and not because she's grieving over their dad. Maybe I'm making a big deal out of nothing, but she's not acting like herself . . . she reminds me of how you used to be."

Cynthia winced. She was glad he was staring at the phone so he didn't see it. She worked to keep her voice calm and steady. "In what way?"

"She seems kind of jumpy and quiet. Sometimes when we're hanging out, she looks like she's lost in a sad place in her head, and sometimes I have to say her name a couple of times before she answers." He looked up to meet her gaze. "When we met for lunch at the diner the other day, she flinched every time the waiter came up behind her and once when the guy at the next booth stood up fast. She even seemed to be constantly scanning the room, even though she was trying to act normal. I'm the one who's been treated for PTSD, and I don't even do that as much anymore . . . She acts like every veteran I was with at the Ranch."

With that, his voice cracked and he took a sip of his pop. As he was about to speak again, his phone buzzed.

His frustration and hurt flowed in his sigh. "She just canceled tonight. No explanation or anything, just said she's sorry but something came up. She says she'll explain later, but she never does."

"That doesn't sound like her. Do you think she would talk to me about it?"

Zachary's eyes widened. "Mom, please don't tell her I said something to you. Let me see if she'll talk to me first."

"Okay." Cynthia got a flash of brilliance. "Hey, I have an idea! Do you remember when you two made those throw pillows for your grandmas for Christmas when you were in high school? She was a natural with a sewing machine back then, and she liked it enough to make a bunch for herself. Do you think she would help me with the Fall Festival fiasco?"

His brows pinched in confusion. "I thought we were trying to get her to talk to you, not work for you."

She chuckled. "Do you remember all those times we worked in the yard together?"

"Yeah."

"And did dishes? And worked on school projects?"

"Yeah." His eyes narrowed, and she could see the wheels turning in his mind.

"Do you remember how much we talked while we were working together?"

Recognition washed over his face. "Ahh . . . You were playing me?"

"I was *relating* to you." She tapped her temple and winked. "Ninja Mom trick."

He laughed and shook his head. "How did I never notice that?"

"Because I was good at it."

"I guess you were. It seems worth a try if you're sure."

"Zachary, this is Laci we're talking about. She's always been special to me, and she's your best friend. Of course I'm sure. We need to try to help her."

Lord, please help us.

Chapter 10

WYATT ADJUSTED THE COLLAR on his shirt and looked around the room. It was his second date with Madison, and they were at the Taste of Fall event at Bellows Vineyards. He usually went with Cynthia, but she said she had promised Mitch and Bella that she would go with them and encouraged him to ask Madison. Why her brother suddenly needed a chaperone, he didn't know.

Bellows Vineyards hosted the annual event and invited other restaurants from the area to bring special dishes that the community could taste and vote on. The vineyard sat on top of a hill in the middle of Summit County with amazing views of the fall colors below, and the food was always delicious. The money raised was used for a good cause, helping fund a local program that taught kids how to garden and then to prepare the food they grew.

Madison was fun and easy to be around, and having an attractive woman on his arm silenced the well-meaning church ladies and townsfolk who so enjoyed mothering him. When Cynthia had secretly invited her to go along fishing when he took her and Zack out a few days earlier, he was pleasantly surprised to see that Madison knew her way around a tackle box and did, in fact, bait her own hook. He'd only asked her out after that to appease Cynthia and get her to stop nagging him about it, but found that he liked Madison enough to ask for a second date without any prodding.

Wyatt and Madison were following the courses in order and were tasting and voting on their favorite salads. As they were laughing about some of the unusual varieties of fruits in the salads, Wyatt saw Cynthia walk in with Mitch and Bella.

He was shocked to see that she was wearing something that didn't look like it came out of her father's closet for once. It still concealed the figure he knew was underneath, but it was nice to see her look like she was almost comfortable being a woman for a change.

When their eyes met across the room, his breath caught. He realized he had been staring, and it felt as if he'd been busted doing something wrong. He looked down and brushed imaginary crumbs from his shirt while he willed the heat to leave his cheeks. As Madison waved her over, he nodded a greeting toward Mitch and Bella.

Cynthia was all smiles. "Hey, you two! Having fun, I see."

Madison greeted Cynthia with a hug. "I'm so glad you made it! And thanks again for introducing us a couple of weeks ago. He's a very talented salad critic." Madison grinned at him and winked.

When Cynthia started looking over the salad table and contemplating her options, he pointed toward a corner of the display. "Stay away from those two, Cyn. They've got pine nuts."

She nodded as she continued to peruse the spread. "Oh, thanks. It's good to have tasters to go before me."

"You don't like pine nuts, Cynthia?"

"She's allergic."

"Ahh, I see."

Despite having no reason to, he was starting to feel awkward standing between the women. He quickly reminded himself that it was Cynthia—his *friend*—who had introduced them and nagged him to ask Madison out. Very forcefully, by the way. "How about if

I get us some drinks while you ladies catch up and compare weird fruits?"

When he got to the bar, Mitch was there ordering drinks for himself and Bella. He smacked Wyatt on the back in friendly greeting. "Who's the date?"

"Someone your sister set me up with."

Mitch coughed and shot a look over at Cynthia and Madison. "Seriously?" He shook his head.

"Yeah, she thinks she's a matchmaker now. Why, is there something I should know?" His job made him look at people with a wary eye, but he hadn't seen any red flags during the time he had spent with Madison.

"About her specifically? I have no idea. In general? Yes." He snickered as he handed some bills to the bartender and picked up his drinks. "See you later."

Wyatt had no idea what Mitch was talking about. *People in love say some weird stuff.*

Chapter 11

LACI PICKED UP SEWING again as if no time had passed, and she was a great help to Cynthia. They had worked side-by-side during two other evenings after Laci got out of work, sometimes in silence, sometimes chatting like schoolgirls.

The topic of Laci's relationship hadn't come up so far, and Cynthia was being strategic with bringing it up. She remembered what it was like hiding secrets and darkness and knew how strong the defenses of a shame-filled woman could be. She wasn't completely certain if Laci was being abused, but her gut told her that there was definitely something wrong in that relationship. Cynthia saw the same sad, faraway look on Laci's face that Zachary had seen, and it was completely unlike the normally joyful girl.

After spending hours praying for Laci in the middle of the night, she got the idea to bring up her own story by talking about Zachary while they worked. "So Laci, how do you think Zachary is doing since he's been back?"

Laci's face lit up and she looked like the girl Cynthia had known since she and Zachary were in elementary school together. Her blonde curls even still bobbed when she spoke. "He seems so much better! He's almost like the old Zack again."

"Sure seems to be."

"I told him he's like the third version of himself."

"How is that?"

Laci paused her sewing and started using her hands as if she were giving a speech or teaching a class. "The first Zack was the boy I grew up with. He was fun and smart and was up for anything. The second Zack, after he came back from Walter Reed, was shut down and quiet, really distant." A look of sadness crossed her face. "I think of that as Broken Zack."

That was fitting. "Thank God he's not so broken anymore. What about now?"

"Now he's still different from the first Zack, but I think in a good way. He's back to laughing and being fun and really sweet, but he's more serious and deep now too. He's more mature than anyone else our age, and gets really excited when he talks about taking classes in January and starting a new business with Mitch to go with the hardware store."

Cynthia smiled, picturing her brother and son working out plans to be business partners. "I think it really helps him to have those future possibilities to focus on. I still worry about him sometimes though. I guess that's my job as his mom."

"I guess so. He's sure a lot better than he was before going to the Ranch. I hated that he would hardly let me see him before he left."

Cynthia shuddered as she remembered the shell of himself Zachary was during the long months between returning from Walter Reed and leaving for the Veteran's Ranch. "He wasn't himself then, was he? He's been asking me a lot of questions about past stuff from his childhood since he got back home. Has he been asking you things too?"

Laci looked contemplative as she went back to guiding the apron skillfully through the machine. "He's been asking me about my dad at times, letting me talk about what it has been like since losing him." Laci's father had died a few months ago after suffering a massive stroke. "I'm still getting used to the idea that he's gone, and our relationship was kind of . . . complicated, so it's really sweet that Zack asks and listens to me. He checked in with me every day during the time that I was sitting with my dad at the hospital, even though he was going through his own stuff at the Ranch."

"He cares a lot about you. Does he talk about his father?"

"Actually, he has." She looked down and focused on the cloth in front of her. "He's talked a little bit more lately about how awful he was to you and how scary it was to grow up with him for as long as he did. He said they told him at the Veteran's Ranch that having childhood trauma like that made him much more likely to get PTSD."

Cynthia felt the familiar hitch in her gut and was not surprised that Laci was avoiding her gaze. She had realized years ago that there would be long-lasting effects on him, but it was always vague and theoretical. Seeing what he had gone through after the IED and how much harder it had been for his mind to heal from that than the other guys who were in the vehicle with him was excruciating.

"I'm sorry, Cynthia." Laci had always been such a sweet girl, and it was obvious how bad she felt about saying something that could cause pain.

"It's okay, honey. I know that his childhood—that my choices—made things harder on him." It was always harder thinking about the effects that the early abuse had on Zachary than telling her own story. She needed to continue steering the discussion though. For Laci's sake.

"What else did Zachary say about him?"

"Just that he was a bad guy and that he's glad that you left him and that he left town."

"That makes two of us." Cynthia saw her opening. *Please, Lord, give me words.* "His father was a bad guy. I hate to say that about someone and I pray for him and hope he got his life together, but he was. And his violent ways harmed his son so badly . . . ."

Laci started to respond, then closed her mouth, as if she had a question, but was hesitant. Cynthia had seen it before when she talked to women, so she rolled along with her story to take the pressure off. "You know, when we first met, Kirk was really sweet. He didn't show his true colors until he knew I had fallen for him and his sweet talk hook, line, and sinker."

Laci paused but stared at the panel while Cynthia continued without missing a beat. "It was love at first sight. Or at least infatuation. You knew he was a teacher and was my cross country coach, right?"

Laci nodded. "Zack told me."

"All of the girls in school had crushes on the new teacher, and those of us on the track team thought we had died and gone to Heaven when we found out that he was going to be our new coach. At first, he was really encouraging about my running and taught me about proper form and pacing. When others weren't around, he told me how beautiful and special I was and how much he wanted to spend all of his time with me." Even after so many years had passed, it didn't seem real.

"He would watch me in the hallways at school and sneak winks and notes to me several times a day. He always wanted to know what I was doing and who I was with when he wasn't there. Because he 'missed' me so much, of course." She rolled her eyes at the ploys to cover his possessiveness as she made air quotes. "I thought no one had ever felt as loved as I did. With his position at the school we had to sneak around, but that made it even more exciting and romantic."

Cynthia continued guiding the panel through the machine, hoping that Laci was taking her words in and that it would seem like she was lost in her story even as she tried not to actually get lost in it. "Of course, the fact that a man in his twenties was interested in a sixteen-year-old and that we had to sneak around and lie should have been red flags number one and two, but I was caught up in the fantasy until it was too late. Even now I'm shocked at how skillfully he started changing. It happened gradually enough that it slipped under my radar, even though the change was dramatic."

"How did it start?"

She's listening. Cynthia tempered her excitement at Laci's question.

"He slowly stopped the sweet talk and started being just a little bit critical, even when he complimented me. I went from the runner he saw promise in to the one who couldn't do anything quite right. Even the physical part started slowly, with an occasional slap or shove. Of course it was always my fault, according to him. He was older, and I believed he understood things better than I did. He eventually had me convinced that he was the only one who would ever put up with me."

Laci's eyes were wide. "Did your parents know? Or do something?"

Cynthia felt the familiar pang of regret. If only she wouldn't have been so good at hiding. "They thought it was good at first too. They always supported our sports and wanted us to succeed. Having my coach spend extra time training me because he saw that I had potential seemed like a good thing. Of course, they didn't know that a lot of that extra 'training' was long walks and kissing on the trails in the woods where no one would see us."

She felt bile rise in her throat as she pictured her younger self, so trusting and innocent, being sucked in. "When the first bruises showed up, they were minor and could easily be covered up or explained away. Running through the woods, it wasn't unusual to scrape against a tree limb or trip once in a while, so . . ." She took a sip of her tea to swallow down the emotion. "Later, when I couldn't put off telling them that I was pregnant, they had a fit—as they should have and I would have if I were in their shoes. They wanted to press charges against him, but I wanted to marry him and have a happy family. By the time I had Zachary I was seventeen and could move out, so I did. That was the beginning of years of misery." Telling her story always exhausted her, but if she could help Laci, she would tell it a thousand times.

"Were there good times too?" Laci's natural optimism was accompanied by a hint of desperation in her tone.

Cynthia laughed sardonically. "If you call 'good times' days when he didn't call me names or accuse me of cheating on him or pull my hair or hit me . . . that became my definition of good days, especially after I had Zachary. As time went on, there weren't a lot of those."

"Why didn't you leave when he hit you?" Laci had shades of anger in her eyes, the accusation Cynthia had seen in the eyes of victims and non-victims alike. Almost everyone got mad at women for not leaving at some point, even the understanding ones and the ones who had been there. Cynthia always chose to answer it as if it were more a question than an accusation.

"Because by the time he first hit me, he had already beaten my spirit to a pulp. That's what they do. I was so primed that the first slap barely registered with me. And I believed him when he said he was sorry and that he wouldn't do it again. Later when he graduated to punches, I also believed him that it was my fault."

Laci's breathing was shallow and she kept her eyes trained on the fabric in front of her.

Cynthia focused on keeping her voice steady. As long as Laci was listening, there was hope. "I'm just thankful that God helped me see that nothing I did was going to turn him back into the man I fell for, because that man didn't really exist. I finally ran out of excuses for his behavior and ran out of hope that he would become the person I was convinced he could be. Thankfully, God and my brother helped me get out before things got even worse or he hurt Zachary too."

Laci stopped, and Cynthia saw that she had struck a chord. *Please help her take this in, Lord.* She didn't want to push Laci too far or make her feel pressured. The last thing that would help would be pushing so far that Laci would defend the guy. *Time for some encouragement.*

"I've learned when I've told my story that it always seems cut and dry to people who haven't lived it. People who have been through it understand that it's much harder and more complicated than it would seem." She took a deep breath, ready to change the tone of the conversation. "Here's the good thing though. There is always hope."

Laci's eyebrows shot up.

Cynthia smiled at her. "You didn't see that one coming, did you?"

Laci laughed nervously. "No, not really."

"Here's the hope. When we get out of the cloud of confusion and shame and fear, we find that everything they told us about our worth and our place in the world was wrong. Sometimes it takes a very long time, but we eventually find out."

Laci seemed to be blinking tears from her eyes. "But what if we're really not worth all that much? What if waiting for the guy who thinks we're special to come around is a waste of time?"

Cynthia smiled at her. "When I start to believe that lie, I open Psalm 103 where it says that God knows we are dirt."

Laci's forehead wrinkled the way it had when she was a little girl and didn't get a joke. "How does that help?"

"Because in the same passage it talks about how much He treasures us."

Chapter 12

WYATT TOOK A QUICK shower after he got home from work, hoping there was time for a short visit with Cynthia before he had to go pick Madison up for their date. It seemed like he'd barely been across the street in the few weeks that he'd been dating again. One of the downsides of having a social life was that it took him out of his normal routine, a routine which he quite liked.

He was enjoying getting to know Madison and they had a good time together, but he wasn't sure how much longer it was going to last. He had been up front from the beginning about the fact that he wasn't looking for any long-term commitments, and she said she was comfortable with that. Most of the women he had dated in the past several years had said the same thing at the beginning though, and it always changed after a month or so. Such was the dating dance, he supposed.

He liked Madison a lot as a person and was inspired by her strong faith and compassion for others. She reminded him of Cynthia in that way.

It was because he liked her so much that he felt bad about taking up her time. She wanted a family someday and since he was not going to be changing his plans any time soon, she should be moving along and finding someone who wanted the same things out of life.

In times past, he would have talked to Cynthia about it. This time was different though, since she had played Cupid with them. It was as if she had her own investment in the relationship.

Checking his watch and happy to see that he had plenty of time, he walked across the street. Cynthia was on her porch with her Bible in her hand and her eyes closed. As he approached, he considered the possibility that she had fallen asleep. He started to turn around.

"Where are you going?" Her smile was gentle and inviting.

"I thought you might have fallen asleep while you were reading."

She looked down at the open book on her lap. "Nope, just praying."

"I saw your light go out as soon as Laci left last night. How is your stealth project going?" He settled himself into his usual seat.

"Good, I think. She seems to be listening and absorbing, at least."

"I can't imagine what it's like for you to tell your story over and over. How do you do it?"

"God helps me. He reminds me that there is hope and that if I can help even one person, it's worth it." She looked down at Roscoe lying peacefully at her feet. "It's a little harder this time though. I've known Laci since she and Zachary were in first grade. She's always been special to me, especially since she lost her mother at such a young age."

Cynthia looked at him with misty eyes. "Her mom was one of the few who didn't look down on me for being a young mother—or a single one, for that matter. She was always gracious and encouraging and never acted like Zachary or I would be a bad influence on her kids."

The look on her face was like a sucker punch. She had never talked much about what her experience had been like as a young single mother, and his heart broke for her.

"Did people really treat you like that?"

She nodded slowly, looking past his shoulder.

"That's awful."

"My mother always reminded me that it's human nature to judge and that God is the only one I'm supposed to look to for approval." She caressed the pages in front of her. "Laci's mother seemed to see beyond the girl who had a baby at barely seventeen. She even whispered in my ear one time that she was proud of me for making the choice to have Zachary instead of other options available. I feel like I owe it to her to help her daughter."

"That puts extra pressure on you when you're talking to her."

She nodded. "It does. Between that and how close she is with Zachary, I can't separate this time. It's even harder filtering out things I don't want him to know when I talk to her."

Cynthia was always careful with details she shared in public because she never wanted anything to get back to Zack that he didn't already know or remember. Wyatt didn't even know many details other than the fact that Cynthia had Zack at seventeen after getting pregnant the first time she had sex and that Zack's father had been abusive to her and left town years ago. The guy was also several years older than her, which put him in an even worse category of abuser in Wyatt's book.

"I know you want to protect Zack, but do you still need to?" He put his hands up in surrender. "I mean that as a question, not a suggestion."

She smiled weakly. "I know. I'm not sure I'm ready to let him know just what a monster his father could be. He doesn't need to know some of the worst details." Tears filled her eyes as she looked down again and pulled her shirt more snugly around herself.

Wyatt kneeled down next to her chair and pulled her into his arms. "You're the best mom and the strongest person I know. If you think it's best to shield him, then that's what you should do."

She held tightly to his neck as a sob escaped her. He wanted to protect her privacy in case any neighbors got nosy, so he slowly stood and pulled her to her feet with him. Without letting her go, he led her inside the house and over to the couch where he sat with her and held her until her tears stopped.

"Thanks, Wyatt." She relaxed against him. "You take great care of me. That's why I wanted to introduce you to Madison, so you can have someone to take care of you."

Madison. He had completely forgotten.

Sneaking a glance at his watch, he saw that he was going to be late. He hoped she was the understanding type, because he couldn't leave Cynthia in the state she was in.

"You take great care of me too. Don't worry about my dating life."

She jerked out of his arms and sat up on the edge of the couch, wiping her tears with the back of her hand. "Your dating life! Wyatt Henry, you have a date tonight. Get out of here!"

He didn't move. "If you need me, I'm staying. She'll understand."

When she stood and tried to pull him up, he gave her a look. "You can't pull me up, or have you forgotten the laws of physics?"

"Maybe you've forgotten the laws of Cynthia." She continued tugging at him. "I'm fine. I got my dose of crying on your shoulder, and now I'm good."

"I'm not leaving you if you need me, Cyn."

"I don't. I'm good, really. Go."

"Okay, okay, if you insist." He slowly stood. "Promise me you'll call if you need me."

"I won't need you, but I promise."

"One last thing." He put his hands on her shoulders and looked into her eyes. "A man should treat a woman like she is the rarest and most precious of gems. I pray that someday you let a real man into your life who will treat you like you deserve to be treated." He pulled her forward and kissed her on her forehead. She deserved everything good. "I love you. Have a good evening."

"Love you too. Tell Madison I said hi." As he walked through the door and onto her front porch, she held the doorframe. "Wyatt . . . Thanks."

He winked and tipped an imaginary hat as he skipped out the door and jogged to his truck, ignoring the knot in his gut. He hated walking away from her when she was hurting. If he thought for a moment that she would let him stay, he would have canceled the date altogether.

Chapter 13

CYNTHIA AND LACI HIGH-FIVED each other when they finished the last of the aprons and hats for the Fall Festival with three days to spare. Cynthia grinned as she filled the tote bag to drop it off at church.

"I don't care if I never see another apron outside of my own kitchen for the rest of my life." She left the heavy bag where it was and made a mental note to ask Zachary or Wyatt to carry it to her car later. "Laci, I don't know how to thank you for all the help you've given me. I never could have finished this without you. Please let me pay you for your time."

"No way! Think of it as my tithe. It was fun sewing again and spending time with you." She looked at the piles of alterations-in-progress. "Do you need any help with the rest of this stuff?"

Cynthia looked at the piles and sighed. "Did those piles somehow get bigger?"

"I think they grew when we weren't looking."

"I really could use some help. How about if I hire you to help me?"

Laci bit her lip as if she was contemplating the offer. "You don't need to do that. Now that Mr. Case made me the office manager at the construction company, I'm making more than enough to get by. Maybe we could make a trade though."

Cynthia's eyebrows raised. "Like a barter?"

"Sort of. I'd like to learn to really sew on my own, not just small projects like pillows and aprons, but clothing too. My brother and I found a bunch of my mom's and grandma's clothes in the attic when we were sorting through it, and there are a few pieces that I would love to repurpose into something fun." Her blue eyes were sparkling, and she bounced in her chair the way she had as a young child. "Would you teach me?"

Cynthia almost squealed in delight. "I would love to teach you! It's a deal."

When Laci's phone buzzed and she looked at the screen, the grin on her face disappeared. "I'm late getting to my boyfriend's, so I have to go. He's already barely speaking to me. See you tomorrow night after work?"

"Perfect. I'm excited that you're going to be back. I've enjoyed our talks."

"Me too." She hurried toward the door.

"Laci?"

"Yeah?"

"Be careful."

Chapter 14

WYATT COULDN'T BELIEVE WHAT he was hearing. So this was why Sarge asked him to come to his office after his shift ended on a Friday when others weren't around. "Retirement?"

"I know I look young, but this job is making me old." Sergeant Ripley sat across from him, looking and sounding as crusty as ever. "My wife and my cardiologist tell me I need to make some changes, and since I like everything about my life except this job, I'm going to do it. I may even follow in your footsteps and buy myself a fishing boat."

Wyatt leaned forward and stuck out his hand. "Congratulations, Sarge. This place won't be the same without you, but I'm happy for you."

"And for yourself?" The look on Sarge's face suggested Wyatt was missing something.

"Sorry?"

"Henry, do you think I'm telling you before I tell anyone else because of my love for gossip? This isn't a beauty shop."

It took a moment for the realization of what he was hinting at to sink in.

No. No way.

"I want you to take my place."

Wyatt's head was shaking before the words came out of his mouth. "No offense, sir, but I'll pass. You hate your job."

"You should have thought of that before you took the sergeant's exam."

"I only took that to shut you up."

Sarge laughed. "I hate parts of this job because I have to deal with people—even worse, cops. Cops are worse than regular people." He put up his hand. "Present company excluded, of course."

"Of course." Wyatt knew Sarge loved every member of the department like they were his own family, but he went along with the usual way he joked about cops.

"You've got the patience for this. I was good on the street, so they gave me the job. You're good on the street, but you're good with cops too. I've seen how you are with everyone from rookies to old veterans like me, and they respect you. You'll be even better in this position than you are in yours."

Wyatt stroked his jaw as he thought about what Sarge was saying. He had grown weary of some of the situations he encountered patrolling the streets—namely, breaking up bar fights and domestic quarrels. Even though those calls were infrequent, it seemed like each time they took more out of him. A job that kept him at a desk more might not be that bad. He had actually enjoyed parts of the administrative work back when he was promoted in the MPs.

A desk job would also take him out of the line of fire more. Cynthia would be thrilled about that, as would his mother.

"Take the weekend to consider it. I haven't told anyone about it yet, not even the chief, and I'm not going to for a couple of days. When word gets out, people will be clamoring for it, but the chief will want my opinion. My opinion is that you're the most qualified."

Wyatt slowly nodded. "I'll consider it, and I'll pray about it."

"Even better. I already asked God to tell you to do it." He stood and reached for his jacket. "Give me your yes within the next few days. The chief will be less likely to try to get me to change my mind if he likes my suggestion for a replacement."

"You're sure about this?"

"As sure as I've ever been of anything. Think about it, pray about it, enjoy the Fall Festival, and tell me yes on Monday."

Wyatt chuckled as he reached across the desk to shake Sarge's hand. "Thanks for the vote of confidence, sir."

His prayer started before he left the building. When he got home, he was disappointed to see Cynthia's car gone. He needed a sounding board for the thoughts slam-dancing in his head, and he'd hoped to at least get her initial reaction before he left to pick up Madison for the movie date they had planned.

The prayer that had started as he walked out of the meeting continued while he showered and shaved. He sat at his kitchen table and jotted down a few pros and cons before sticking the list in his pocket and heading out the door. Cynthia would certainly help him to sort it out later.

Chapter 15

CYNTHIA GATHERED UP PLATES and cups from the tables in the big tent. She was glad she had volunteered for the chili cook-off at the Fall Festival since she didn't have Wyatt to go places with as much lately. It was easier having some type of job when she went to things alone. Wyatt had asked her to go with him and Madison, but she didn't want to be a third wheel and was trying to give them space so they could see where the relationship would go.

When she had the idea to set her best friend and permanent plus-one up with someone, she hadn't thought about how it would drastically change her life. She missed him. He seemed to be enjoying himself though, and that was her main goal.

She looked across the open space just in time to see them walking through the craft show area. When she saw Madison casually loop her arm through Wyatt's, she felt a pang of jealousy. *What must it be like to be so carefree with a man you're dating? What must it be like to date someone like Wyatt, strong and trustworthy?* As if the sight burned her eyes, she turned away and dumped a stack into one of the trash bins.

In some ways, she envied Madison. It seemed like she was the type of woman who would even be comfortable on first dates. The last time Cynthia had felt comfortable on a first date was when she went to the Homecoming dance in tenth grade. Her date was a boy she liked from her English class, and he was a gentleman who treated her with respect. They dated for a few months after that and had a nice time together, but the relationship eventually fizzled out.

Unfortunately, she met Kirk soon after, and he took her breath—and her senses—away. He was charming and handsome, and he said all the things a sixteen-year-old girl wanted to hear. If only she had known he would take her self-respect, innocence, and sense of safety too, maybe she would have made different choices. If she had followed her gut instead of her naiveté, she never would have gone on the trails or anywhere else alone with him.

The one good thing that came out of the nine years with him was Zachary. He was the best son a mother could ask for.

Zachary made up for every bruise and harsh word, and then some. If making different choices would have meant losing the honor of being Zachary's mother, she would go through it all again. Of course, she didn't need all those years or all that heartache to know what kind of man Kirk was. She learned everything she needed to know about his disregard for her feelings and his willingness to overpower her to get what he wanted on the night that Zachary was conceived. If only she would have gotten out then and raised Zachary alone from the beginning.

"Cynthia!"

She jumped when she heard her name called, but smiled when she saw Laci running toward her.

"Hi, Laci!"

"Wow, these aprons and hats actually look great!" Laci scanned the area, satisfaction in her eyes. "I thought it was silly that they were going to have everyone wear them, but they look really nice on them."

"They do, don't they? If it wasn't for you, about half the workers in here would be covered in chili. You did a great job."

"Thank you!" She looked across the tent at the various containers on the table. "I can't wait to taste the chili. My brother and I are going to have our own contest to see who can eat the hottest ones. He and Brianna are waiting for me over there, but I wanted to say hi." She gave Cynthia a tight hug before bopping off to meet them, and Cynthia breathed a sigh of relief as she waved to Garrett and Brianna. *One more afternoon that she's not with the one who is probably hurting her. Thank God for brothers.*

She watched them walk away as she started clearing another table. Cynthia's own brother was just a teenager when he made himself a human shield to protect her and Zachary and get them to safety. He had shown up to return the basketball pump at just the right time to prevent a beating that might have been her worst. Even her last.

She had just declared that she and Zachary were moving back in with her parents for good and had started packing their clothes. The rage in Kirk's eyes as he tore the suitcase out of her hand was worse than she had ever seen, and she was afraid he would kill her. He had certainly told her enough times that he would do that before he would let her leave him. She should have believed him and should have moved out while he was out of town for work. Looking back, Mitch was still a child himself when he walked into that house, but as he ushered her and Zachary to safety, he walked out a man. She would never forget what he risked for them.

She shook her head to get out of the memory. Spending time talking about her history with Laci was bringing old memories and feelings far too close to the surface.

A glance at her watch told her that her volunteer time was over, and she carefully took off the apron and hat and hung them on the rack she'd set up for them. Strolling through the carved pumpkin exhibits, she took in the fresh air and the activity around her. The catapult was ready and waiting to fling pumpkins into the bay, and she chuckled, remembering how much Zachary had loved that as a little boy.

"Hi Mom."

She startled at the sound of Zachary's voice. "Whoa, where did you come from?" She was so lost in thought that she hadn't noticed him walking up beside her. "I was just thinking about how much you used to love the catapult when you were little."

He grinned as he watched the activity around the big contraption. "I have to admit I still love it just as much. I planned my lunch break around this today."

"Perfect timing." What a change from last year. Then Zachary was still getting used to the prosthetic leg and was struggling with nightmares and anxiety, so he didn't go to the Fall Festival or many other town activities. He went to work and spent the rest of his time in his room. She had even had to beg to get him to go with her to their traditional Thanksgiving and Christmas gatherings with friends and family.

"Hey, Wyatt!" Zachary waved Wyatt and Madison over before Cynthia saw them or had a chance to make herself scarce.

When they got to where she and Zachary were standing and delivered hello hugs, Wyatt whispered in her ear, "I need to talk to you later."

"Sure, I'll be home."

He had the look on his face that he always got when he had something weighing on his mind. She wondered if he wanted to talk to her about Madison. Maybe he was finally ready to take a step of faith and get into something long-term.

An unfamiliar pang hit her stomach. Suddenly the busyness of the day and stress of thinking about the past caught up to her, and she wanted to go home.

"Well, guys, I think I'm going to head out. It's been a long day. A long week, really."

Wyatt's face fell. "What about ax throwing? I've been waiting all day for you to finish your shift." He turned to Madison to explain. "We have a long-standing contest. She won last year, so I need to reclaim my manhood this year."

Cynthia chuckled. "You can have your manhood back. Maybe you can try to beat Madison."

"You can't just give manhood, Cynthia. It's not a participation ribbon. It has to be earned." He put his arm around her and squeezed her as he put on a pleading face. "Pleeeease?"

"You're pathetic." She sighed with all the drama she could conjure up in her tired state. "Fine, I'll beat you in ax throwing again. But then I'm going home."

Zachary snickered at the two of them and nudged Madison. "These two never change or grow up. I hope you're cool with that."

Madison laughed. "I find them pretty entertaining."

Wyatt started flexing and stretching his right arm while he stared Cynthia down. "Just stretching."

"Yeah, and I'll have the ice pack ready for you later, Hercules."

Chapter 16

Wyatt gratefully accepted the ice pack Cynthia handed him from her freezer a few hours later. When she pulled the lid from the crock pot, the smell of apples, cinnamon, and cloves filled the air even more than when he had first walked in a few minutes ago. The first mulled cider of the fall was always the best, and Cynthia made it better than anyone.

He inhaled, savoring the scent. "I don't know why you insist on waiting until the Fall Festival to start making mulled cider. Next year I'm going to replace all of your calendars and trick you into making it early."

"You forget that every year I let myself get conned into doing something for the Fall Festival, so I always know when it is." She ladled the cider into his favorite cup, then into hers, and handed both cups to him.

He carried them into the living room and set them on the coffee table, then started a fire. By the time she walked in with a plate of oatmeal raisin cookies, the fire was roaring.

"When did you have time to make cookies?"

"While you were voting on pumpkins and taking your date home. I hope you don't mind if they're a little warm." She winked as she set the plate in front of his usual chair.

He grinned and reached for a cookie. "You're the best thing about this town, Cynthia."

"Aww, thanks. After the ax-throwing debacle, I needed to do something to make myself feel better."

He gestured toward the ice pack he was holding on his aching shoulder. "It was worth this to get my manhood back."

She shook her head and stared into her cider. "I didn't even let you win. I can't believe I was so off today." She raised her mug. "Here's to next year."

"Don't rush things. To my victory." He sipped the cider slowly and savored the warmth and perfectly blended flavors. "This might be the best mulled cider you've ever made."

"Same recipe as always."

"Perfect recipe. Is there anything you don't do well?" He put his free hand up. "Actually, don't answer that. I don't want the mystique broken."

She smiled as she reached for a cookie.

He set his mug down and leaned forward. "I need your input on something."

Her eyebrows raised, and she looked almost fearful for a moment.

"It's nothing bad. Sarge pulled me into his office yesterday to tell me he's retiring . . . and that he wants me to take his job."

Cynthia gasped. "Wyatt, that's wonderful! You passed the sergeant's exam years ago, and you would be great at it."

As he had thought and prayed about it over the last twenty-four hours, he hadn't realized how much he hoped she would think so. "I think I want it. You saying that confirms it."

She smiled and bowed her head with a flourish. "You're welcome. But what did God say about it?"

Wyatt scratched his chin. "He showed me that a lot of what Sarge hates about it are things that either wouldn't bother me or I might enjoy. There are also things I would definitely hate though."

He took a bite of his cookie. "I asked Him to use you to tell me if I was off my rocker for considering it."

"Well, let's ask Him together." She put her mug down and clasped her hands.

As they sat there praying together for his decision, and then for Zack and his healing, then for Laci and her courage, time seemed to stand still. He loved praying with Cynthia because once they started, they kept going and covered everything until God told them to be done. Sometimes it lasted a few minutes and other times, like when Zack was going through his rough patch, it lasted hours.

When they raised their heads and their eyes met, she looked different to him. She always had a peace about her after they prayed, but that wasn't it. It occurred to him that it wasn't just his job that kept him out of serious romantic entanglements—it was Cynthia too. If he was involved with someone, he wouldn't be able to spend the time he did hanging out at her house and talking or praying until all hours of the night with her. As it was, he had missed her during the time he'd been spending with Madison.

Maybe if he took the new job, he could balance that better and not feel like he was losing out on something. He needed to find a way, and he would do just that.

Chapter 17

CYNTHIA WAS DRAINED BY the time she turned the lights off. Looking across the street, she saw Wyatt in his favorite chair with his head bowed. He was probably talking to God more about his job decision. She prayed again for his wisdom and thanked God for the friend and prayer partner she had in him.

If only I would have met someone like him when I was sixteen. Shaking the thought from her head, she rechecked the deadbolt on the front door and went to bed.

It was her habit to pray for the people she loved as she drifted off to sleep. She always started with Zachary and her parents in case she fell asleep fast, usually followed by Mitch and Wyatt, then whoever God brought to mind.

While she was praying again for Wyatt's wisdom in making his decision, she realized that his reason for staying single would be lessened if he took the job. She pictured him with Madison earlier in the day at the Fall Festival. They seemed to enjoy each other and have an easy time together. It was just what Cynthia wanted for him and why she had introduced them.

Tears came out of nowhere. They poured out of her as she mourned for her loss of ability in the relationship department. Zachary, her dad, Mitch, and Wyatt were the only men she felt completely comfortable around and the only ones she could even imagine herself feeling safe with.

She felt another pang of envy as she pictured some of the women in her life and their freedom to fall in love. She prayed for every woman-in-love she could think of, starting with Mitch's girlfriend, Bella, and the brides who were bringing dresses to her for alterations. Even if she didn't get to experience such things for herself, she could enjoy the happiness of others from the sidelines and cheer them on.

The next day she woke up with a new prayer focus for Laci. She prayed as always that she would have the courage and strength to get out of the relationship she was in. Going further, she asked God to heal her enough to trust herself to love again, to let someone wonderful and kind love her the way she deserved.

Cynthia pictured Zachary and chuckled as she realized that when she prayed for spouses for Zachary and Laci, she always pictured them with each other. *If only they would see it. Lord, if You wanted to bring them together, I wouldn't argue with You.*

She might not be able to have a relationship, but she could pray for others. At least there was that.

Chapter 18

WYATT LEAFED THROUGH THE policy and procedure manual Sarge had just handed across his desk. It was always nerve-racking to start a new position, and reading manuals was not his favorite thing to do. Regardless, he felt a sense of peace about taking the job and was actually looking forward to it.

"Congratulations, Henry. You're going to do well, and the department is lucky to have you."

"Thank you, sir. I appreciate your confidence."

"Now get out of here. It's Friday night, and you've earned a relaxing weekend."

The week since Sarge first approached him about the position had been a hectic one. The chief had quickly agreed with Sarge's recommendation and given him the promotion, and he had started training that morning. He would be transitioning into the new job over a month's time so that it would be smooth for both him and the department. It would also give them time to hire and train his replacement.

Cynthia had insisted on throwing a small party for him tomorrow night to celebrate the next phase of his life and career, and Madison had insisted on taking him to the Birchwood Inn for a more intimate celebration in an hour. When he noticed the clock, he closed the binder. "Sarge, you're right. If I don't leave now, I'm going to be late for my celebration dinner."

"Good, that means I can leave too. Have a great time, and I'll see you on Monday morning."

He went home and took a quick shower to get ready for his date. His phone buzzed with a text from Madison just as he was walking out the door. She said she was running late and asked if they could meet at the restaurant instead of at her house. Having time to spare, he walked across the street to chat for a few minutes before leaving.

He found Cynthia in her sewing room. "Do you notice anything different about me tonight?"

Cynthia looked up from the blouse she was mending and studied him. "Should I?"

"Yes, you should. My brain is noticeably bigger after all the studying I've been doing all day."

"Oh, that." She smiled. "Of course I noticed that. I thought maybe you were wearing something new for your date or something."

He looked down at the shirt Cynthia gave him for Christmas two years ago. She had always said it brought out the different shades of blue in his eyes. "Why would I get something new when I have my favorite shirt?"

She tilted her head as she eyed it from different angles. "I'm seeing a little bit of wear on that one. I guess I know what I'm getting you for Christmas this year."

"Thanks a lot for spoiling the surprise." He pulled out his best pout.

"Don't worry, I've already gotten a few things for your stocking. I promise there will be surprises."

He wiggled his eyebrows. "I hope you got some of my favorite socks again. I'm ready for some new ones."

"Noted, but that's between me and Santa. Aren't you going to be late?"

"We're meeting at the restaurant." He looked at his watch and saw that he'd been there longer than he realized. "And I have to go. Have a good night."

"Be careful. Love you."

"Love you too."

When he arrived at the restaurant, Madison pulled into the spot next to his. He hurried to open her door for her. "Great timing. You look great, as always."

"Thank you. And you look very handsome. I love that shirt on you."

"It helps to have a professional fashion person buy my clothing."

She turned quickly and started walking toward the restaurant. "It's more chilly than I realized. Let's get in there and see if there's a table open by the fireplace."

There was, and the meal was delicious. He didn't go to restaurants much, but it was a nice treat to go to a place where they cooked his steak exactly as he liked it. After they finished their meals, she started fidgeting with her napkin.

"Is everything okay?"

As she was about to answer, the waiter appeared out of nowhere. He disappeared just as stealthily after taking their plates and setting the bill on the table.

She reached for it quickly. "This is my treat, remember? We're celebrating your new life."

"My new life. That sounds big." *Really big.* He took a swig of his Coke. "Thank you again."

"Yes, your new life. This is a great chance for you to think about what other changes you might want to make."

She took a deep breath and looked into his eyes. He wondered if what usually came after a look like that on a date was coming.

"I'm so glad Cynthia introduced us, Wyatt . . . and I think this should be our last evening together."

Didn't see that one coming. "Oh? Why is that?"

She reached over and squeezed his forearm. "Because you're a great guy and I don't ever want to be the other woman."

Other what? His brain twisted in confusion. "Other woman? I'm not dating anyone else."

Her laugh surprised him. "You're not, but you should be."

"Sorry, I'm not following." *Sometimes I hate being a guy. We miss a lot.*

She reached back across the table and put her hand on his. "Wyatt, please don't take this wrong. You're a smart guy, but you are dumb as a stump when it comes to matters of love."

He just stared at her, unsure what the proper response was to being called dumb in such a kind manner.

"Do you really not see it?"

Apparently not. "See what?"

"That you and Cynthia are basically an old married couple who still have the spark but live in separate houses."

He felt the heat rise in his neck and squirmed in his seat. Cynthia was family to him, like a sister—at least that's what he had told himself over and over again through the years.

He shook his head as he prepared the standard response to such suggestions. "We're good friends, that's all."

She smiled and straightened in her chair, the way someone would if they were preparing to explain something to a child. "Okay, let me ask you something. When did you talk to Cynthia about the promotion?"

"The night after Sarge brought it up." *Because she wasn't available twenty minutes after you got the news yourself.*

"When did you tell me?"

He rubbed his face with his hands. "The day after I accepted the position."

"Exactly. You're married." Her voice held no judgment. She was simply stating facts.

"I'm sorry. I'm just so used to talking to her first." That would likely never change either. Cynthia would always come first.

"Don't apologize. The heart wants what it wants, right?"

He felt like a jerk. "I'm sorry. I've enjoyed our time together and didn't mean to give the impression that something was going on."

"I've enjoyed it too, and we said from the beginning that we weren't starting something serious or long-term. I also saw from the beginning that you two had something special that you were both apparently blind to, even though I ignored it." She put her hands up. "No regrets here."

He folded his napkin and set it on the table. "Is this the real reason we drove separately?"

She laughed when she nodded. "And the reason I chose the night I was paying. I knew you would feel guilty cutting the conversation short if I had paid the bill."

He chuckled and shook his head. "You are good. Very crafty. Remind me never to negotiate against you in a real estate deal."

"Actually, remember that you would do well to have me on your side if you're ever negotiating a real estate deal. I'm definitely smoother than Cynthia was when she introduced us. I'm trying to return the favor." She smiled warmly. "I've never known two people more connected who hadn't been married for twenty years. You and Cynthia and Zack are a family, Wyatt. Go make it official."

"She's not exactly open to relationships either."

She shrugged and stood. "So change her mind."

Chapter 19

CYNTHIA RAISED HER HANDS and threw back her head in victory. "Yes!"

Mitch threw his cards on her dining room table in mock disgust. He and Bella were the last people remaining at the party. Even Zachary had left to go out with friends.

Wyatt grinned at Mitch. "That's what happens when you play at the big kids' table."

"Come on, Bella. Let's get out of here before she wins more favors from me. I already have to rake leaves and clean her gutters."

Bella laughed and added her cards to the pile. "You think that's bad. I have to sweep up her sewing room!"

Cynthia chuckled. "You'll appreciate that clean floor when you're in there getting a wedding dress altered." When she saw both Bella and Mitch blush, her chuckle practically turned into a cackle. It seemed she'd accidentally hit a nerve.

Mitch kicked her under the table and snuck a glare at her that told her everything she needed to know about his intentions. Her baby brother was planning a proposal very soon. She was sure of it. As he and Bella stood, she realized she needed to change the subject quickly.

"Mitch, you didn't mind our wagers so much when you had me scrubbing the floor at the hardware store. I'll see you on my lawn soon."

When he kissed her goodbye, she whispered, "Sorry."

"You didn't break any news. She knows it's coming. We're waiting for *your* announcement."

He laughed at her quizzical expression and ushered Bella out the door.

She watched them walk to Mitch's truck, wondering what he was talking about. "My brother says some strange things sometimes."

"Blame it on the love. He said something to me a few weeks ago at Bellows Vineyards that I still haven't figured out."

She chuckled as she gathered the cards from the table and put the rubber band around them. "It's nice to see him so happy."

"It is. She's a great match for him." Wyatt looked around the empty room. "Well, as usual I'm the last guest to leave. Thanks for a great party."

"You're welcome. I'm sorry Madison couldn't make it. I hope she's feeling better soon."

He scratched his jaw. "Yeah, we kind of lied to you about her being sick."

Cynthia stopped and looked at him. "What do you mean, you lied?"

"We decided to stop seeing each other last night and didn't want you to feel bad."

She chastised herself for feeling a ping of relief, then felt sad for him. "I'm sorry." She had hoped he would find happiness, even if it meant less time with him. "Was it the usual 'we want different things' discussion?"

"In a way." The way he looked down at the floor suggested that there was more to the story, but he would tell her when he was ready.

Chapter 20

IF YOU ONLY KNEW. He wanted more time to pray and process what Madison had said when she broke it off with him before bringing the subject up with Cynthia. In the twenty-four hours since their dinner, he had thought and prayed about little else.

Madison was right, and there was no denying it. The relationship he had with Cynthia was different than what he had—or wanted—with anyone else. If he was looking to marry and build a life with someone, it could only be her.

The thought of pursuing a relationship with her had nagged him like a summer gnat since he moved across the street from her ten years ago. She was everything he would have looked for if he was looking.

But he wasn't looking. And neither was she.

His decision to forgo getting married and having a family helped him keep his attraction to her locked away in the back of his heart, but she was the only one who ever made him question his life choices. If she would have shown any interest over the years, he would have quit his job immediately and dug ditches for a living for the chance to be with her.

"Hello?" Cynthia was staring at him with her hands on her hips. "I asked you a question while you were off on another planet."

"Sorry, just thinking about something."

"Hi. Welcome back to Earth." She pointed to his chair in the living room and walked in there herself. "You've been acting like something was on your mind all night. What's going on in there?"

You. The dam has been broken and you are rushing through my mind like a flood-stage river.

She sat in her chair and stared at him. It felt so foreign to keep something from her. He talked to her about everything, and she always helped him to see things differently and know the right choices to make.

This was different though. This was risky. He rubbed his neck as he paced in front of the fire. Realizing he was acting suspiciously, he sat in his chair.

Cynthia studied him, then let out a slow breath. "Oh, wait a minute . . . Wyatt Henry, did you get your heart broken?"

Worse. I got it woken up.

"No. That relationship just ran its course like it always does. We both walked away injury-free."

She studied him for a long moment. "Why does this seem different then?"

"I've just got a lot on my mind. Can I ask you a question though, now that you've taken such an interest in my love life?"

"No, you may not set me up with anyone."

"Got it." As if he could ever let another man near her. "Do you ever think about dating again?"

Even in the dimly-lit room, he saw the flash of panic on her face. "No."

"Why not? You're not a vulnerable sixteen-year-old girl anymore. You're an intelligent, independent, beautiful, strong woman. You wouldn't fall for another creep."

She looked at him like he had just suggested she flap her arms and fly to the moon. "Have you not heard me all these years? I have a son to focus on, and I don't need or want a man in my life."

Something propelled him to keep talking. "I'm not sure if you've noticed this, but your son is twenty-three years old and is as mature and self-sufficient as anyone I know. Your parenting was successful enough that you worked yourself out of a job."

She looked down, but not before he saw the tears that sprang to her eyes. He silently prayed as he gave her time to answer.

Finally she spoke, but her eyes were firmly stuck to the blanket she'd pulled onto her lap. "I wouldn't know how to date even if I wanted to. I will admit I've been feeling very envious of Madison lately though. Seeing how relaxed and confident she was around you made me wish I could be someone else."

He stood up and pulled the Ottoman in front of her chair. Sitting down across from her with his knees bracketing hers, he took her hands in his. "Please don't be someone else, Cynthia. You're perfect as you are."

She finally looked up at him. "You're my best friend so you're supposed to say that. I can't even imagine feeling comfortable with a man."

"Thanks."

She chuckled and squeezed his hands. "You know what I mean. You don't count. You're safe."

Well you're not. Not anymore.

He took a deep breath, trying to slow down his heart as it pounded wildly in his chest. *Lord, tell me what to do here.*

Without realizing what he was doing, he blurted out the words he'd promised himself he wouldn't say yet. "Madison says you and I are married."

Chapter 21

CYNTHIA INHALED SHARPLY. SHE was sure she misheard what Wyatt said. "We're what?"

"Married. She says we're an old married couple who live in separate houses."

Her heart started racing. Suddenly the hands that were clasped in his felt as warm as her cheeks. The laugh that escaped her lips sounded as nervous as she felt.

"Why would she say that?" People had made teasing remarks about their relationship for years and they had always shrugged it off, but this felt different.

This time, his eyes weren't laughing. They were searching. "Do you think she's right?"

She had no answer. Or breath. She couldn't think of him like that. It was too dangerous. "Do you?"

He pulled his hands from hers and counted on his fingers as he spoke. "We talk to each other about everything. We only make big decisions after consulting with each other. We cry on each other's shoulders. We pray together. We have more fun and make each other laugh harder than anyone else could. We kick butt in every game we team up together for. We finish each other's sentences and read each other's thoughts." He stared at his fingers, as did she.

When his gaze returned to meet hers, he looked different, like he was scared but summoning his courage. "You're the one I want to talk to about important things, share good and bad news with first, and spend my time with. So yeah, I think she's right. I haven't needed or wanted a wife for all these years because I had one living across the street."

Over the years that she had fought feelings for him, she had convinced herself that the case was closed. Now he had just ripped it open. She didn't know what to do.

This is dangerous.

He took her hands in his again. "You're shaking."

She could only nod. For the first time in all the years she had known him, she had no snappy comeback for him, no profound wisdom to offer. She had nothing but fear.

He had just stripped away all her defenses, everything that made her feel safe in her small corner of the world. With a few words and a yearning in his eyes, he had awakened a hope and desire in her that she thought she had killed years ago by her wrong choices.

"Cyn . . . did I just mess things up?" His eyes were tearing up. "I had to say something, but if I lose you because of this, I don't know what I'll do."

Tears filled her eyes too, and she hung onto his hands as if she were drowning and they were her lifeline. She wanted to run from the house, but more than that she wanted to crawl into the arms that were inches away.

She felt like she was paralyzed. All she could do was stare at him while tears pooled in her eyes. "You will never lose me." She barely recognized the voice coming out of her mouth. "But I don't know what to do with this."

"I don't either. I've been trying to make sense of it since Madison brought it up. My head has been spinning, and it's been killing me not to talk to my best friend about it."

She reached over to pick up the box of tissues and put it between them on her lap. They sat there crying together for a long moment.

She chuckled softly. "We're sitting here crying and blowing our noses together with no shame or dignity. Maybe we are an old married couple."

He reached his arms out to her and she fell into the bear hug that had always comforted her. Her emotions were a jumbled mess by the time she pulled back.

Standing slowly, he reached out his hands. She let him pull her up and lead her to the couch, where they sat together side by side, hand in hand.

"We don't have to talk more about this tonight if you don't want to. Just please don't make me go home yet. I need to know that you're okay and that I didn't scare you off or ruin what we have."

She could feel his eyes on her and turned to meet his gaze. "I'm afraid to mess with what we have. I love you and I'm afraid to risk letting it become more, as wonderful as that could be."

"I am too. But I can't deny the way I feel about you anymore—not to myself and not to you. I love you like family, but as much as I've fought it all these years, I have to admit the truth." He took a deep breath without breaking her gaze. "I'm in love with you."

She swore she could hear music playing in the back of her head. Having him look at her that way and tell her he was in love with her was more than she ever let herself dream of or want. The part of her heart that had been locked away and buried for years screamed to be set free.

As if it was the most natural thing in the world, she reached out and put her arms around his neck. It felt good to hold him and to be held. He wasn't hugging her as her friend this time though. He was the man who had just told her he was in love with her. And she still felt safe in his arms. More than that, it felt right to be there.

"I love you too, Wyatt."

He loosened his grip on her just enough to look into her eyes. "Those are the greatest and most terrifying words I've ever heard."

Chapter 22

A WEEK LATER, WYATT took Cynthia's porch steps two at a time. He didn't remember a time when he felt like he was walking on air. No wonder people said and did such weird things when they were in love.

He and Cynthia hadn't talked about their relationship since he had so awkwardly told her he loved her, but their time together had been different over the last few days. There were times when silences were more charged and times when the usual teasing and banter took on a sweeter tone. It was as if they both just fell into step with the new direction their relationship was going.

He held the picnic basket in front of himself as he waited for her to answer her door.

She grinned as she held it open for him to come in. "Since when do you knock?"

"Since I've come to ask you for a proper date. I figured I should be a little more formal."

Still grinning, she blushed and looked away.

Suddenly feeling like a teenager, he shuffled his feet. "Am I allowed to do that? I know most people date first, then fall in love and we did things the other way around, so I'm completely confused about how to proceed with this relationship."

"Me too. Come in." She looked down at the picnic basket. "Are you here to ask for a date that starts right now?"

"Umm, sort of." He looked at her sheepishly. "I'm not very good at this yet. Also, I was being spontaneous."

"Well, I'll be. Here I thought all these years that you didn't have a spontaneous bone in your body."

He grinned as he gazed down at her. "It turns out I just needed the right inspiration."

"And it turns out that I don't have any appointments and don't feel like cleaning the house today, so yes, I would like to go on your spontaneous date." She glanced at the clock in the mantle. "Can we be back by five? Laci is coming over."

"No problem. I was just thinking that since the sky is blue and the sun is shining, we could take a drive to look at the fall color." He patted the picnic basket. "When we get hungry, we can pull over somewhere with a pretty view and eat lunch."

"That sounds like a very well-thought-out spontaneous plan."

As they drove around Summit County, they took in the beauty surrounding them. Country roads that went on for miles over hills and around curves were the perfect passageway, and it was as if they were enveloped in the red, yellow, and brown leaves themselves.

"I guess I shouldn't be surprised that a cop would know more back roads than a lifelong resident, but I'm still impressed."

"Are you hungry? There's a dead-end two-track road up here that has a great view of Sapphire Lake."

"Sure!" She took in the scene with wonder as he parked the truck at an angle that gave them the best view of the lake from the tailgate.

While he slowly unpacked the picnic basket, she looked at him suspiciously. "Why do you have that look on your face that says something is on your mind again? I thought this was a spontaneous drive."

His lips twitched, and he tried not to trip over his words. "It was a spontaneous drive, but I was wondering if I could talk to my old pal for a few minutes. I need some dating advice, and she's the one I usually go to."

She straightened her shoulders and tossed her hair. "Okay, your old pal is back. What can I help you with?"

"Well, I've got this girlfriend now and—"

"Girlfriend, huh? That was quick." She cocked her head in feigned bewilderment. "But wait, I thought she was your pseudo-wife."

"If I'm honest, I'm hoping she'll be my real wife someday, but I'm not going to rush that." He couldn't help but laugh at the way she coughed and blushed. "Anyway, as you know, she's incredible. The thing is, sometimes I think she looks like a scared kitten, and it makes me wonder if I've messed up by pushing the relationship. She seems to get over it pretty quickly, but I wondered if you have any advice about how to help her."

She looked like she was about to make a wise-crack, but instead paused and grew serious. "I think she's just getting used to things. It's a big change for her, and she hasn't been on a date with a good guy since she was a teenager. It seems to me that you're doing great."

He ran his hands through his hair. "Well that's a relief. I don't want to scare her off."

"You probably won't, but maybe don't propose to her just yet."

"Okay. So next week?"

She giggled and leaned over to kiss him on the cheek, sending his heart rate soaring. He had been afraid to hug or kiss her even in the friendly way he used to since they had their talk a week ago, and he missed her touch.

"That's another thing. Do you think it's okay if I hug her or kiss her? I used to get to do that—you know, safe brotherly hugs and kisses—but now I'm kind of afraid she'll think I'm trying to get away with something or move too fast."

The smile she shot him was beautiful. "I can assure you that she appreciates that. And that she misses your bear hugs."

"Well, all right!" He reached over and pulled her into a hug and kissed her cheek. "You're the best friend in the world. Can I have my girlfriend back now?"

Chapter 23

CYNTHIA COULDN'T PRY THE grin off her face if she tried. Their last stop was her favorite scenic lookout over Lake Michigan.

It was south of Hideaway and set high on a hill that towered over the lake. The walk up to the top required several flights of stairs, and they took their time to look out over the lake at each landing. They were both a little out of breath by the time they reached the top, and she was glad that none of the other people there had ventured that high. It was as if the place was theirs alone. Clouds had moved in since they had started their day, but the sun was still peeking through enough to color the big lake with all shades of blue.

As she stood with her hands on the railing looking down at the lake, he walked up behind her and put his hands next to hers. It felt good to have him so close, and she leaned back against him. "This is a nice almost-hug. It doesn't feel very brotherly though."

"But it's still okay?"

"More than okay. You're safe, remember? I trust you to hug me."

"Those words are music to my ears. I'm always going to work to earn your trust, you know."

She turned around so she could put her arms around his neck. "You already have it."

It felt like the most natural thing in the world when he wrapped his arms around her waist and kissed her forehead. "Then I'm always going to work to keep it."

She rested her head on his chest and sighed. "This is the best date I've ever been on."

"Me too. I love you, Cynthia."

"I love you too." She looked up into his eyes. They were so full of tenderness as they searched hers. She had never seen that look on his face, but knew him well enough to know that he was looking for permission.

Tilting her face up and smiling, she parted her lips ever so slightly. When he met them with his, it was different from anything she had ever experienced.

The first kiss she had as a teenager was with her Homecoming date, and it was awkward and fumbling. The first kiss with Kirk was intense and possessive, even frightening.

Wyatt's kiss was soft and tentative. His wasn't demanding anything of her. It was just a sweet expression of love that she was more than eager to return. His kiss made her want to stay in his arms forever.

She drew back and smiled at him. "That's the best first kiss I've ever had."

"Me too. Maybe that's because we're both with the right person this time."

"That must be it. What do you think the second one will be like?"

He pulled her tightly to him again. "Let's find out."

When they finally got back to Cynthia's house, Laci and Zachary were sitting on the porch. As they approached the steps, Zachary had a curious look on his face and he and Laci were exchanging glances and giggles.

"Hi Mom."

"Hi Zachary. What are you up to?"

"I could ask you two the same thing."

She and Wyatt shared a look. "I have no idea what you're talking about." *He knows. He's reading us like books, and he knows.*

She wondered if she should have talked with him about it, but then she reminded herself that they were both adults and that neither of them had to ask permission from the other about how they spent their time.

When Cynthia and Laci started walking into the house, she heard Wyatt ask Zachary to stay on the porch with him for a few minutes. She could guess what he was going to say, but the two of them had their own relationship and it was their business.

When she and Laci got into the workspace, Laci turned to her with a big smile on her face and spoke in a conspiratorial whisper. "Is something finally going on with you and Wyatt?"

Cynthia's face betrayed her, and she broke into a grin. "Well, I haven't talked to Zachary about it."

Laci hugged her and giggled. "Zack knows. He's always known, and he can tell something is up."

Always? She couldn't stop herself from asking the question burning in her mind. "And is he for or against the idea?"

"Oh, he's totally for it!" Laci's blue eyes danced in excitement. "He told me that when he told stories about you two at the Veteran's Ranch, he just referred to you as his parents because it was easier than trying to explain your friendship."

Cynthia chuckled as she walked over and turned on her sewing machine. "It seems that everyone but us knew."

"It seems so." Laci started fumbling with the fabric in front of Cynthia's machine, making no move toward her own chair. "What made you change your mind about dating?"

Cynthia smiled contentedly as she pictured Wyatt's face. "The right person. Wyatt has shown me who he is over years of time. He's a good man who loves God, and I know he will never hurt me. I also know that I can trust myself to recognize good character again, and I trust him." She looked up and met Laci's gaze. "We all deserve people like that in our lives."

Chapter 24

WYATT WIPED HIS PALMS on his jeans as he sat on the chair Laci had just vacated next to Zack. He was almost as nervous for this conversation as he had been last week with Cynthia. The stakes were high, and he prayed it would go well.

Zack stared at him and scratched Roscoe behind the ears while Wyatt tried to figure out the words to say.

"There's something I need to talk to you about."

Zack looked like he was using all of his strength to keep a serious face. "Are you going to finally ask for permission to date my mom?"

"Maybe blessing would be the word. What do you think about it?" He knew the odds were in his favor, but still held his breath as he waited.

"It's about time! I think you can make her really happy." Zack paused, then laughed. "Of course, if you hurt her, you know I'll kill you."

"It goes without saying." He stuck out his hand to Zack. "Your blessing means everything to me. You know that, right?"

Zack grasped his hand and gave it a firm shake before laughing again. "Do I have to call you Dad?"

Wyatt's laugh was filled with relief. "You call me anything you want. Thanks, Zack."

The next day, Wyatt went with Cynthia to her church. Even though he preferred his and wasn't crazy about the way Cynthia had been taken advantage of by some of the people there, it was her church home and his place was by her side.

Madison approached them at the end of the service with a smile on her face. "Is this what I think it is?" She motioned between the two of them with her perfectly manicured finger.

He looked at her sheepishly, still feeling uncomfortable with the whole situation. "You were right."

Cynthia hugged her. "Thank you for what you did. Are you sure you're okay with this?"

"Of course I am! I'm happy for you." She started to step away, but looked back with a wink. "But next time you set me up, can it be with someone who isn't in love with you?"

Cynthia's face went rosy. "Next time."

They only had a few minutes to socialize before they needed to leave so they could get to Evelyn Glover's place for lunch. Evelyn went to a different church, First Community, but it let out shortly after Cynthia's. Evelyn and her late husband had been friends with Cynthia's parents for decades, and she was like a second mother to Cynthia. Just like several others in town, Cynthia and Wyatt often went to her house for meals and for many of the special celebrations she hosted throughout the year.

As they approached the door to leave the church, Cynthia turned back to gaze around the sanctuary with a look on her face that seemed to be a mixture of sadness and hope.

"Are you okay?"

She nodded. "I'm good. I think this is goodbye here."

"Really?" As much as he disliked some things there, he hoped she wasn't saying that on his account.

"Really. There was a time for this place to be my church home, but I would like it if we found a new place that fit for both of us."

He slipped his arm around her shoulders. "I would like that too. How about next week we try First Community?"

"It's like you read my mind."

It wasn't unusual for them to have lunch at Evelyn's on a Sunday, but it felt different showing up there as a couple. Cynthia had obviously filled Evelyn in on their status change, because she enveloped them both into a hug when they arrived.

"I'm so happy that you two finally found each other." She kissed them both on the cheek. "You were right under each other's noses for so long."

Wyatt squeezed Cynthia closer. "We know, we know. I had to convince her to give us a shot."

"And I'm glad you did." Cynthia's smile was the most beautiful thing he had ever seen. How had he lived for so long without her at his side like this?

No matter. She was there now, and if he had any say in it, would be forever.

Evelyn's big, beautiful Victorian home was a bed and breakfast, but the guests were out on fall color tours, so it felt like a typical family and friends gathering. It was Zack's Sunday to work at the hardware store, so Mitch was there helping Bella set the table. Bella had moved into a small room upstairs after the apartment she had been renting over someone's garage closed up for the winter, and she had taken to helping Evelyn out as much as possible. Evelyn's niece, Shelby, lived there too, and she and her fiancé, Clay, were bringing food in from the kitchen. The smell of chicken and dumplings filled the large dining room and made his stomach growl.

When Mitch approached them, he made the same lame attempt that Zack had made at looking serious. As if there was a chance he wouldn't approve. After hugging Cynthia, he grasped Wyatt's hand. "You finally got it. What took you so long?"

There was no point in trying to defend himself, so Wyatt just laughed in response.

Mitch leaned in, puffing out his chest. "You know what happens if you do anything to hurt her, right?"

"You'll have to race Zack to get to me, but yes, I'm well aware of the beatdown I'll get."

"Good." Mitch gave him a hearty slap on the back. "Welcome to the family, brother."

Chapter 25

CYNTHIA ROLLED HER EYES and laughed at her baby brother's tough guy act. When she had told him a few days ago that she and Wyatt were dating, he had snickered and said that he had been waiting for that announcement for years.

Mitch glanced back toward Bella then lowered his voice as he leaned toward Wyatt. "Can I borrow my sister for a minute?" Without waiting for an answer, he pulled Cynthia toward the parlor, his excitement palpable.

"What's going on?"

"I need your help." He pulled her farther into the room, checking over his shoulder like he was afraid they'd be followed. "Do you have any time to go shopping with me this week? I've got Bella's potential engagement rings narrowed down to three possibilities at a couple of antique stores, but I want to pick the perfect one."

"Most definitely!" Cynthia hugged him tightly. Despite him being ten years her junior, she had always had a special relationship with him, especially when she and Zachary moved back in with the family after getting away from Kirk. She had even taken to mothering him at times in his teenage years when their parents weren't able to be as active in their late-in-life child's sporting events and activities.

She had prayed for years for him to find someone like Bella and couldn't wait to help him find a ring as unique as she was. Ideas for a wedding dress for the woman who had exchanged her previous wardrobe of designer fashions for unique thrift store finds when she moved to Summit County started flowing through Cynthia's head. She would wait to be asked, but since Bella had already brought several items to her to be altered, she was pretty sure her help would be welcomed.

"Good. We've talked about getting married in the spring, but I want her to have time to plan what she wants. I'll let her call the shots since she didn't get much say in her first wedding—or marriage, for that matter."

"I'll help in whatever way I can."

"Thanks, sis. I knew I could count on you." As they started back toward the dining room, he whispered in her ear, "Any chance for a double wedding?"

Her cheeks became warm, and she felt a knot of fear in her stomach. "Don't get your hopes up. We're not rushing."

Marrying Wyatt would be a dream come true, but she wasn't sure if she was ready for that yet. She was still sorting out the conflicting feelings she had when she was with him. She had never been happier in her life, but prior experience had taught her to be wary of relationships and especially of physical intimacy. The stirrings she felt when she kissed Wyatt—or even thought about him—were more wonderful than anything she had ever felt, but they still made her uneasy, and she wasn't quite sure what to do with them yet. She definitely needed time.

Chapter 26

OVER THE NEXT COUPLE of weeks, Wyatt and Cynthia got into a flow with their new relationship. Not one person was surprised when they announced that they were dating, and several were confused by it because they thought they already were.

Wyatt was just glad to be out in the open with his feelings for her and to spend even more time with her now that he wasn't wasting his time dating someone else and had a more consistent work schedule. They started going to church together, and First Community fit what they were both looking for as well as they had hoped it would. They both knew Pastor Ray and had so many good friends among the congregation that it was a natural place for them to start their life together. Zack went with them when he wasn't working, and with Mitch and Bella attending as well, it truly felt like a family affair.

Cynthia's parents, Mitt and Connie, were coming from Florida for Thanksgiving, and even though Cynthia wasn't ready for a proposal yet, Wyatt had prepared his speech so that he could have "the talk" with them while they were there and they could do it in person.

Even though he had known them for years and they treated him like a part of the family, he was still nervous about approaching them. The whole family was protective of Cynthia after what she had been through in the past, and he wanted to make sure he had their full blessing. Though Zack, Mitch, and Cynthia's sister, Sarah, had all extended theirs, he didn't want to assume he was a shoo-in with Mitt and Connie. Cynthia made her own decisions, but he knew it was important to her to have their support. He intended to do anything to get it.

Chapter 27

CYNTHIA SAT AT THE kitchen table and watched Wyatt wash the dishes. She'd tried to help, but he had insisted she sit and relax after she had prepared their special one-month anniversary meal. The meal itself was a compromise. She got the china and crystal place settings that she wanted because it was a special occasion, and he got the pot roast that had sentimental meaning as the first meal she had cooked for him.

The evening felt as special as the relationship. She had even put on one of the dresses that she had made for herself but never worn. Maybe now that she had someone who she felt safe and comfortable with, she would finally wear her treasured creations instead of shoving them into the back of her closet after finishing them. Her designs were modest, but they didn't provide the camouflage that her ill-fitting sweatshirts and jeans gave. She had made the dresses for her own enjoyment and never thought she would have an occasion or the comfort to wear them in front of anyone.

Even sitting in her kitchen with Wyatt, the man who had her heart and who she planned to spend the rest of her life with, she still felt a bit self-conscious in the pretty dress and had an urge to cover herself with a sweater or at least a shawl. She resisted, determined to push herself out of her comfort zone and to feel okay with wearing something pretty, for both Wyatt and herself.

She watched him as he took special care with the china. It reminded her of the special care he had always taken with her. Wyatt was very good with fragile things. "You know, I could get used to this kind of service. You're going to spoil me."

He smiled and winked. "I have every intention of doing just that. You've been spoiling me for years." He patted his not-quite-flat stomach. "You're responsible for about fifteen pounds of this, you know."

When the last dish was dried and put away, she ladled out the mulled cider and put a piece of apple crumb cake and a dollop of homemade whipped cream on each of their dessert plates. After setting their desserts on the coffee table, she made herself comfortable on the couch and watched him build a fire in the fireplace. Now that she was allowing herself to look at him as a man and not just a neighbor or a best friend, she was rather enjoying the view. The warmth she felt while watching him was even getting more familiar, as was the way she reacted every time he touched or kissed her.

When he finally joined her on the couch, she lifted her blanket so he could share it. They sat in blissful silence as they ate their crumb cake and watched the fire.

She smiled up at him. "I like our new regular seating arrangement."

He put his plate down and put his arm around her. "Me too. I could sit here like this with you every night for the rest of my life."

"Me too." She put her plate beside his so she could snuggle under his arm. "I still feel safe with you, Wyatt."

"I hope and pray that you always will." He squeezed her close against him, her new favorite place to be. "You look so beautiful tonight. I've always wondered if I would ever see you in one of the dresses you made."

Heat crept into her cheeks. "I was hoping you would like it."

"Like it? I love it!" He leaned close to whisper in her ear. "Of course, I knew you had those curves under your bulky clothes."

His confessional tone made her giggle. "How did you know?"

"I am a man, you know, and I have eyes. Every once in a while when you bent or reached for something, whatever huge garment you had on would hug you in parts." He put up his hand in surrender. "I promise I didn't gawk, but I couldn't help but notice."

"I like not feeling like I have to cover up in front of you."

"I hope you never do."

After the years of having Kirk insist that she put her body on display for him and have it available for his use and abuse, she had gone far in the other direction after leaving him. It was her best effort to feel safe and protected. Wyatt's presence itself made her feel safe and protected, and his show of desire for her was no threat. Her own desires for him kept her awake at night, and she longed for the day when they could live together as a married couple.

She wished she could encourage Wyatt to propose to her and that they could get married right away. Something was in the way though, and she wasn't ready. She knew it had nothing to do with Wyatt and didn't understand it, but she asked God again to reveal it to her.

When she finished praying and opened her eyes, Wyatt was looking down at her and smiling. "Praying?"

She nodded. "For us."

"Perfect." He kissed her on her cheek, then her nose. She giggled as he finally got to her mouth, and she pulled him closer. Kissing him was one of the best parts of her days lately.

Time seemed to fly when she was in his strong arms. Everything was good there, and she knew she would treasure every moment with him for the rest of her life.

She was giving herself fully to the kiss—to him—when he tightened his hold on her. In an instant, passion turned into threat.

Without permission or warning, her mind took her to days long past.

She was trapped. She needed to escape.

Her heart raced, and she felt the sweat start on her brow as she scrambled for safety.

Chapter 28

IN THE MIDDLE OF one of the best kisses of Wyatt's life, Cynthia suddenly pushed against him and shot out of his arms like a bullet.

Moving from his arms to the end of the couch, she grabbed at the blanket and pulled it around herself.

His heart dropped into a pit in his stomach. She looked like a caged animal.

When he instinctively reached out to her to comfort her, she recoiled from his touch. She sat frozen, face expressionless, eyes wide.

He knew that look. He had seen it time and again on domestics. It never would have occurred to him that his law enforcement training would need to come into play on a date with the woman he loved, but he was thankful for it nonetheless. Trying to give her a sense of safety, he slowly backed toward his end of the couch, holding her gaze.

Her eyes were glazed over, and she didn't look like herself. He tried to keep the fear out of his voice as he choked out his words. "I'm sorry, Cyn. Are you okay?"

She buried her face in her hands and shook her head. There were no sounds coming from her, and he could barely hear her breathing. His heart raced as he watched her sit as still as a statue.

This wasn't like a domestic call. He wasn't the protector coming to save someone from a threat this time.

He was the threat. He was the cause of her pain.

Lord, please help her. Please surround her with Your arms and peace. Please stop whatever is happening to her.

She finally looked up at him with red, despairing eyes. When she finally spoke, her words tumbled out in a hoarse whisper. "Wyatt, what have we done?"

The next morning, Wyatt poured his coffee in silence and stared out the window at Cynthia's dark house. He hadn't slept a wink after she asked him to leave. Amid his tossing and turning, he had spent the night praying and trying to understand what happened. He lost count of how many times he had replayed every second of their evening, especially those leading up to her pushing him away.

It was clear that she was reacting to things from her past, but he had no idea what he had done to trigger it. They had agreed that kissing was the only thing they would do, and neither of them had pushed the boundary lines they set. She had gone from kissing him like she couldn't get enough of it to getting as far from him as she could.

And looking at him like he was a predator.

He couldn't live with himself if he hurt her. All he wanted to do was protect her, treasure her, love her. Instead of those things, he had scared her away.

He slumped down in his recliner and pleaded with God for help. "Lord, I don't know what happened last night, but You do. Please help Cynthia. Please give her healing and peace and a sense of safety with You. I only know a small bit of what she went through, but You know it all. You saw every violent act and heard every unkind word. Help her to remember that You got her out of that and that she is safe now. Please show me how to help her."

His chest tightened. "Lord, please don't let me lose her."

Chapter 29

THE WATER IN THE shower was cooling down. Cynthia didn't know how long she had been in there, but it must have been a very long time if the hot water heater was empty. She looked down at her arms and legs again.

No marks, no bruises. Those were just dreams.

She had cried herself to sleep soon after Wyatt walked out the door. The nightmares started almost immediately and continued until she finally got out of bed at five. After getting out of the shower and making coffee, she sat in the dark and stared across the street at his house for at least an hour as she rehashed what had happened on what was supposed to be their special night.

From her chair she could see him moving around in the kitchen while he made his own coffee, and he appeared to be moving as slowly as she was. He sat in his living room with his mug and Bible and often held his head in his hands.

That's not the man who chased you and hurt you in your dreams last night. He's safe and he's good.

She wanted to rush across the street and get one of those bear hugs he was so good at. She wanted to tell him how sorry she was. It was she who had asked for space though, and she wasn't going to play with his emotions. Her own needed to be sorted out before she did anything.

If only she could talk to her best friend Wyatt about her boyfriend Wyatt. He would know what she should do. He would also give her a big, comforting, safe bear hug and let her cry into his chest.

Since she was wide awake, she walked into her workroom and tried to get started on her orders. It was a good day to be working alone. She was in the middle of a few alteration projects and was designing a funky party dress for Bella. She looked across the room at the wedding dress she was redesigning for Shelby Montaugh. *I'm sorry, Shelby. You don't want me working on your dress today. I might curse it.*

After reminding herself that she didn't believe in curses, she placed the dress behind the changing screen so she didn't have to look at a reminder of the future she had just lost. She looked for easy projects that required all of her focus but not much thought. It had been a long time since she had felt this way, but she knew better than to try to do anything too complicated.

When she walked back to the kitchen to make more coffee, she stopped and looked over at Wyatt's empty house. He had left earlier than he ever did, probably to give himself something to do other than think about how she had freaked out on him and ruined their special evening. As she had always done, she prayed for his safety and wisdom while he was at work. *Thank You, Lord, for giving him that desk job and lessening the hours he's on the street. Thank You for keeping him safe.*

Please tell him this was not his fault.

"You're getting an early start."

She jumped at the sound of Zachary's voice behind her, almost spilling coffee grounds on the counter.

"Sorry, I didn't mean to scare you."

"It's okay, honey. I'm just a little on edge. I hope I didn't wake you."

He walked over to her and gave her a tight hug like he had when he was a young boy. "Not this morning. Are you okay?"

She tried to sound natural as she sat down at the table. "Of course. I just couldn't sleep and decided to get an early start."

He hesitated as he reached into the cupboard and pulled out a coffee cup. "I heard you last night."

Oh no. "I'm sorry. I hope I didn't wake you then either."

He slowly turned and faced her. "It's okay. I've woken you up with nightmares enough over the last year. I prayed for you when I heard you and put you in God's hands."

She stood up and wrapped her arms around him again. "You're a good man, Zachary."

"My momma taught me to take things to Jesus." He winked at her. "I didn't always do it then, but I do now. Can I make you breakfast? I don't have to be at work for an hour."

"That would be wonderful. Thank you, honey."

"Is there anything I can do?"

She sipped her coffee. "Just breakfast."

He nodded and turned to the refrigerator to gather supplies for scrambled eggs. She could see questions forming in him, but she had never poured out her heart to him before and wasn't about to start now. Even though he was a twenty-three-year-old man, he was still her son and didn't need to be her sounding board or support system.

"I'm going to get dressed, then I'll come set the table." Walking into her room, she went straight to the drawer where she kept Dad's old sweatshirts. There was something extra comforting about having a piece of him with her when she felt down. Baggy sweatpants that would be comfortable to work in completed the ensemble. She felt a tear in her eye when she noticed the dress hanging over the chair where she'd left it in her haste to get back into safe clothing after Wyatt left. Quickly putting it on a hanger and moving it back to its previous place in the back of the closet, she stopped and considered putting it and all of the other dresses she had made for herself into a bag to take to the shelter.

She was not as ready to be a woman as she thought she was twenty-four hours ago. Maybe she never would be.

Refocus. This is not the time. She closed the closet door, wiped her face, practiced a smile for Zachary, and walked back to the kitchen.

After going back to work and hunching over her sewing machine for a few hours, Cynthia felt like she was a hundred years old. It was past time for a break. She couldn't do that on no sleep like she used to.

She wasn't hungry, but she took a couple of bites of the scrambled eggs she'd barely touched at breakfast. Pulling out her notebook and sitting by the fire, she wrote about what happened with Wyatt, then about the past. When she filled a page, she balled it up and threw it into the fire.

It wasn't a shock anymore when old memories came up, and at least now she knew what to do with them. Writing them down got the ugliness out of her, and letting the paper burn in the fireplace was a tangible way to let the memories go.

She caught herself looking at Wyatt's house often, and it reminded her what an integral part of her everyday existence he was. He was everything to her. What would she do if she lost him? The thought sent a shudder through her.

"Oh, Lord, please fix me. You are the ultimate Healer, and You work all things for good. I know I just ruined the romance, but please make this better and save our friendship."

When her phone buzzed, she was disappointed to see that the message was not from Wyatt. She wished she hadn't told him to give her time and wait for her to contact him.

It was Bella, asking if she could come over and talk about the dress Cynthia was making for her. She knew a fake excuse for a visit when she saw one but appreciated the gesture nonetheless. Bella was a good listener and wouldn't push her to talk, so Cynthia accepted the offer. It would be a relief to get out of her own head for a while.

Chapter 30

THANK GOD THIS WEEK is over. Wyatt pulled his coat off the hook and paused. Every day for a month, he had grabbed it and shoved his arms into it so fast that he had to remind himself not to pull the hook out of the back of the door. The last week was different though. Instead of looking forward to going home, or more accurately, looking forward to going to Cynthia's after he got home, he was going to an empty house and staying there.

The sleepless nights were getting to him, and he was glad that he had tomorrow off. He didn't know what he was going to do with a whole day of free time, having caught up on all the little projects from his to-do list with his new open evenings of late. He would need to find something. Keeping his hands busy was the only thing keeping him sane.

When he got home and walked through his back door, he re-flexively looked through the kitchen and living room to Cynthia's house. He still hadn't figured out what had happened a few days ago. All he knew was that he had messed up in a big way. He had never felt so powerless in his life.

By sheer force of will, he had honored her request to give her time and not to contact her. For years his days had been peppered with text messages back and forth with her, but there had been none for almost a week. It was the loneliest week he could ever remember, and he had come to understand what the term "heartache" really meant.

When he had spoken with Zack, he carefully avoided the topic of Cynthia other than asking how she was doing. Every day the answer was the same, that she was okay. Zack looked torn every time Wyatt asked, and Wyatt didn't want to put him in an uncomfortable position, so he left it alone.

Exhausted, he stretched out on the couch to try to read. When he finally gave up trying to focus, he closed his eyes and promptly fell asleep.

The sound of the knock on the front door and Zack's voice as he walked through it jolted him out of the nap. He bolted upright and was ready to spring to his feet. "What's happening?"

Zack put his hand out in a calming gesture. "At ease, soldier."

Wyatt grunted. "I'm a Marine." The usual joke between them was the first moment of levity of his day so far. No, his week.

Zack laughed, but then his brow furrowed. "Enough is enough, Wyatt. I'm not going to stand around and watch my mom suffer like this anymore."

Wyatt blinked and rubbed his eyes as he tried to fully wake up. "I suppose you're here to kill me now."

Zack's eyes clouded over, and he let out a heavy sigh as he sat on the edge of the chair opposite Wyatt.

Wyatt threw his hands up. "I'm sorry, Zack. I don't know how I did it, but I hurt her."

"No you didn't. He did." It looked like the idea of killing someone for hurting Cynthia didn't sound half bad to Zack at that moment. "This is all because of him, not you."

"Well, I triggered something the other night. As much as it's killing me to stay away from her, I'm trying to give her the space she asked for." He rubbed his face with his hands. "How is she?"

"Better now than a few days ago. At least last night she wasn't crying or yelling in her sleep."

Wyatt buried his face in his hands. *Oh, Cyn.* "It's been that bad?"

"She's better than she was at first. Mitch and I have checked in with her through the day all week. I've gone home for lunch, and Bella and Evelyn have gone over to see her a few times."

"I don't suppose I'm in a position to say this, but thank you. It's been killing me all week to not be able to talk to her, but she needs space."

"She needs *you.*"

Wyatt looked at him with weary eyes. "Do you have any idea how badly I want to believe that?"

"Well, you need to." Zack's gaze was intense, and Wyatt couldn't look away. "I don't know what happened last week either, but I haven't seen her act like this in years. She won't talk to me about it because she still tries to protect me. She's trying to pretend that she's back to her normal self, but she's a terrible actress. Please go talk to her."

"I'm not sure she'll want to see me, but if you think it will help, I'll try. I can't sit here knowing that she's there hurting."

"Thanks, Wyatt." Zack stood and walked across the room with determined steps. "I'm going over to see Laci. It's time to have a talk with her."

"Be careful there."

"I will, but I have to do something. I don't want to see her end up like my mom."

Wyatt grasped his shoulder. "Can you wait a minute so we can pray for them first?"

"Sure."

The two men stood there together and prayed for the women who had been hurt so badly to be healed and for their own wisdom in talking to them. As they finished, Zack opened the door, then paused. "Thanks for taking care of my mom, Wyatt."

Chapter 31

When Cynthia glanced out the living room window and saw Wyatt walking up the steps, she breathed a sigh of relief. She had been afraid she had scared him away for good after practically kicking him out last week. With each passing day, she missed him more and felt more unsure of how to reach out to him.

When she opened the door, she wished she could hug him like usual, but she didn't know what he was thinking of her at the moment.

"Hi." She clutched the door for support.

He looked equally nervous with his hands stuffed into his jeans pockets. "I'll leave if you're not ready to see me."

She had been ready and longing to see him for days. Her thoughts and memories had been shifting from the bad ones with Kirk to the good ones with Wyatt, but she felt too embarrassed and unsure of what to say or how to contact him. She stepped back and held the door open for him to walk through. When she closed it and locked it behind him, she pulled her long sweater tightly around herself.

After a short silence that felt like days, they spoke in unison. "I'm sorry."

His red eyes looked like he had gotten even less sleep than she had all week. "I promise I'm here as Friend Wyatt. I've spent all week kicking the soup out of Boyfriend Wyatt for hurting you. Are you okay?"

She couldn't stand the guilt she saw on his face. "You didn't do anything. It was me." Tears filled her eyes for the hundredth time of the week. "I'm sorry. I haven't known what to say to you or how to apologize."

He reached his arms out tentatively, and she rushed into them, burying her face in her special spot against his chest. They stood there for a long moment while she savored the safety and peace she felt with him. Her grip on his sweatshirt was so tight that even if she wanted to, she couldn't let go.

He rubbed her back as he spoke softly. "Cynthia, I'm so sorry. I don't know what I did, but I never want to do it again."

She stepped back and led him by the hand over to the couch. They sat on opposite ends, as they had the night everything had gone so wrong. Not knowing where to begin or what to say, she asked God to help her find words.

Wyatt spoke first. "Did I mess up by pushing the relationship?"

She answered as honestly as she could. "I don't know."

"I never want to be the cause of the look I saw on your face that night. If we have to hold off on kissing or even go back to being neighbors who pretend they're just best friends who aren't in love with each other, I'll do whatever. I just don't want to lose you."

Oh, thank God. "I thought I had lost you. I wouldn't blame you if you didn't want anything to do with me after the way I freaked out."

He reached out and took her hand. "It would take a lot more than that. This was the longest week of my life, and it only confirmed that I don't want a life without you."

"I don't either." She caressed his thumb, feeling centered again for the first time in a week. "I went back to my old therapist the other day. She said that trauma reactions like I had aren't that uncommon."

"Can she help you?"

She nodded. "We're going to do some things to work on the issues and memories that came up again. I'm going to go twice a week for a few weeks to get a jump start."

"Good." The look in his eyes was like a warm blanket around her shoulders. "I'll be praying, obviously, but if I can do anything to help, just tell me how."

She fidgeted with her sweater as she gathered courage. She needed to give him the explanation he deserved. Taking a deep breath, she forced herself to talk. "There are things I have to tell you—hard things that I don't like to talk about. You have to know why I reacted the way I did that night."

"Only if you want to tell me."

"I want to tell you. I need to tell you." She took a shaky breath. "You know that I never go into detail about my relationship with Zachary's father because I don't want those details to get back to him or give anyone reason to make any judgments about Zachary based on his biology."

"Yes."

"He remembers hearing us arguing and being scared of Kirk. He's said he has vague memories of hearing me scream, but he's not sure if those are memories of when we lived with Kirk or of hearing when I had nightmares later. I'm thankful that even though I know they're seared into his soul, his memories are vague."

She stopped and took a few breaths to gear herself up for what was next.

When Wyatt caught her eye, she saw concern on his face. "Cyn, it's up to you if you want to keep going. We don't have to do this right now."

His gentleness fueled her resolve. "I do have to do this. You need to know more details before you decide if you want to continue this relationship, because as much as I thought I was past it, it's obviously still affecting me."

"Okay, but can I say something first?"

"Sure."

"Thank you. I just want you to keep in your mind that there's no decision to make about this relationship. Whether we get to continue where we were going or have to go back to being platonic friends, this relationship is here to last. I'm not going anywhere."

She knew he meant it and felt the weight start to lift from her shoulders. Knowing that nothing she had to say would make her completely lose him gave her courage.

In an effort to focus, she kept her eyes on her lap and started from the beginning. "When I met Kirk, I was what I now recognize as a normal insecure sixteen-year-old. He was what I now recognize as a master manipulator and a predator. I mean really, what normal twenty-five-year-old man is interested in a teenager? I don't care how developed she is . . ." She shook her head in disgust. It took a moment to push aside the anger and go back to her story. "He spun a fairy tale in front of me and I soaked it up like a sponge. I was completely blind to how manipulative and controlling he was until I was too far in."

Wyatt listened quietly, never letting go of her hand or taking his eyes off her.

"I know that I've told you that part and you already know that he was my track coach. I'm just trying to work myself up to what else I have to tell you."

"Take your time. I've got all night."

She took a deep breath as she prepared to tell the part of her story that she usually kept to herself. "I've only told two people this, but you need to know . . ." She took a long sip of water, willing it to calm her. "Zachary was not conceived because I wasn't strong enough mentally to rein in my desires . . . It was because I wasn't strong enough physically to stop Kirk's."

It had been years since she had spoken those words to anyone, and it was no easier saying it to Wyatt. Her eyes focused like lasers on their clasped hands. She knew in her head that he had deep compassion for women who had been mistreated, but she couldn't risk the chance that she would see accusation or blame in his eyes.

"Oh, Cyn. I didn't realize . . . ."

She stifled the sob that almost escaped at the care in his tone. "I know. I always figured it was better to let people believe I made a bad choice than to have them think that Zachary—" Her throat froze, unable to finish the sentence. She would die before she would let anyone think Zachary was anything like Kirk or that he was somehow less valuable because of the circumstances of his conception. She kept her eyes down and kept talking, afraid she would lose her nerve if she didn't say it fast. "Kirk insisted that I was making a big deal out of nothing. He said that he could tell that I wanted it as badly as he did and that we had gone too far for him to stop. I had no experience or any way to know anything different. I was confused and ashamed and didn't know what to do or think. He was older and more experienced, and I looked up to him and trusted him. It wasn't until years later that I called it what it really was. Or called him what he really was."

She shook her head, trying to distance herself from the old feelings. "I tried to break up with him, but he said we were eternally connected because of that act and said we would always be together. He also made it clear that he wasn't going to let me go so easily. Of course, I realized I was pregnant right away. That changed everything. He was furious and blamed me, especially when the pregnancy brought the relationship to light and cost him his job. I was stuck with him but tried to make the best of it. I never told anyone what really happened because I thought it was my fault for being alone with him and letting things go as far as I did. I even tried to get my parents to give me permission to marry him."

Wyatt's breathing came in shallow puffs. She felt the tension in his hand but kept her eyes focused on the couch so she could keep talking. "I even convinced myself that we were going to live happily ever after when I moved into his apartment later. I thought it would just take some getting used to and that he would get over being mad, but almost as soon as Zachary was born, I knew there was going to be trouble. If he cried too much or spilled something or just needed attention, it was my fault. If I was tired, it was my weakness."

The warmth of Wyatt's hands on hers gave her strength to continue. "That was when the physical abuse ramped up. I was scared and exhausted and didn't want to admit to my parents how bad things were. I felt like I had created the bad situation I was in. I was too embarrassed to crawl back to them, and he was all I had. No matter how bad things were or how much he resented parenthood, I thought I would be harming Zachary if I took him away from his father. I was trapped, and Kirk knew it and took full advantage."

When she finally dared to sneak a glance at Wyatt, she saw only compassion in his eyes. It fueled her to finish the race she'd started. "Kirk's career as a coach and teacher were done when the school found out about us. Word spread, and he couldn't get another job. Also my fault, of course. When he found out about a job as a long-haul trucker and took it, I knew it was an answer to prayer. He was gone for a couple of months at a time, and during those trips Zachary and I lived in peace."

Those days were precious. She could enjoy being a mother, and Zachary could act like a child without fear. Even then she knew she could raise Zachary without Kirk. "I even prayed that Kirk would find someone else while he was away and leave us, but he kept coming home. When he was home, I sent Zachary to my parents' house—here—as much as I could in an effort to protect him and appease Kirk. I thought I could manage it, and to some degree I did. The one thing I'm proud of is that even though he was afraid, Zachary never got any of the beatings."

"Because you took them for him." His words sounded like they were choking him.

She nodded. "I didn't have much of a choice. The most important thing to me was being a good mom. Kirk resented Zachary because he took my attention away from him and he wasn't my only focus. When he was home, he wanted meals on the table, quiet in the apartment, and free reign with me, not necessarily in that order."

It took all her strength to keep the tears at bay. Focusing on the purpose for telling him her secrets helped. "What happened the other night was me being taken back to those days."

Wyatt reached across and slowly lifted her chin to look at him. His face was red but his eyes were gentle. "Sweetie, I'm so sorry."

Her tears seemed to find a new well from which to draw as she remembered how wonderful everything with Wyatt was before it all went so wrong. "I don't know if I can have a normal marital relationship, Wyatt. I was so happy being in your arms and kissing you the other night and—"

"Do you think that's the only reason I want to marry you?"

"No, but that's a pretty big deal in marriage and it's reasonable to have expectations. I don't want you to be disappointed."

"Cynthia . . ." He held her gaze. "I would walk through fire for you. I would take a bullet for you. I have self-control and a lot of practice at living like a monk, so I'll be fine."

"Are you sure?"

He squeezed her hand gently and smiled at her. "If I don't get to second base by our fifth anniversary, I'm not going to implode."

She half-laughed at his attempt to lighten things up. "I know, but it's different when someone is sleeping next to you."

"I'm not saying it will be easy or pleasant, but I'll manage." He lifted her hand and kissed it before lacing his fingers through hers. "I want to marry you so that your face can be the first thing I see in the morning and the last thing I see at night. I want to share a life with you, not just a bed."

Relief washed over her, and she moved over to sit next to him. It felt good to have his arm around her again. Safe and good.

He gave her a playful nudge. "Wait, we do get to share a bed at some point after we get married, right?"

She nodded and smiled. "Most definitely. I'm not saying we won't have a physical relationship or that you have to wait five years for second base. I don't want to live like a monk either, especially if I have you sleeping next to me. I just can't give you a timeline for when I'll be ready to set a wedding date or able to be comfortable with physical intimacy. Can you handle that?"

"I can and I will, if that's what happens. You are more than worth the wait." He turned her face up to his. "I'm not like him. I will always respect your 'no' and will stop on a dime if you tell me to. Always. You can hold me to that."

If it weren't Wyatt speaking those words, she wouldn't have believed them for a second. But Wyatt had spent the last ten years showing her that he was a man of his word. She knew she could trust him. "Thank you for not giving up on me."

"I'll never give up on you. Don't give up on me either, okay?"

"Never."

She nestled under his arm and rested her head on his chest. For the first time since things went so wrong a few days ago, she felt safe and relaxed. Within minutes, she was asleep.

Hours later, Cynthia woke with a start, which woke Wyatt with a start too. She didn't know how long they had been sleeping in each other's arms on the couch, but it was dark in the house.

"Can you reach that light?" She hoped he didn't notice the quiver she heard in her own voice.

He reached up, and soon the room was filled with a soft glow. The concerned look on his face told her he'd noticed her voice too.

"Sorry. I've been jumpy all week. I kept having nightmares that he came back and—"

"Cyn." He took her hand and sat quietly for a long moment with the look he always got when he was contemplating something. "He's not coming back."

"I hope not. I stopped expecting it years ago, but it all started again last week."

"I'm not sure you get what I'm saying. He's not coming back. Not anytime soon, anyway." The firm tone in his voice suggested he wasn't just speaking reassuring words.

She sat up and looked at him. "Do you know something I don't know?"

He nodded. "I've been keeping tabs on him for years. An old buddy of mine from the Corps is a private investigator, and he has a permanently-open case."

It took a moment for what he said to sink in. He had been monitoring Kirk, protecting them, all this time. "You did that for us?"

"You're kidding, right? There was no way I was going to let him do anything to hurt you or Zack. He didn't change his ways when he left Hideaway, and his current address is in a correctional institution in Idaho. He's not eligible for parole for another six years."

"Wow. I guess I shouldn't be surprised." She leaned back against him.

"Some people don't change. And in case you're wondering, that is the one and only secret I've kept from you over all these years." He rested his head on hers and stroked her arm. "You're safe."

I'm safe.

Chapter 32

WYATT WOKE UP ON Thanksgiving morning with a smile on his face. *Ahh, yes. Turkey, mashed potatoes, Evelyn's apple pie, and football with my family. And I don't have to leave early or show up late because of work.*

Of course, the best part of the day was being able to spend it with the people who made his life worthwhile. He hoped he would wake up next to Cynthia by the next time Thanksgiving rolled around.

Evelyn Glover's long-standing tradition of filling her grand house with people on Thanksgiving started years before Wyatt moved to Hideaway, and he had been part of the regular crowd along with Cynthia and Zack for several years. This year felt different though. Everything felt different, really. The sky and lake took on a deeper shade of blue, the leaves on the trees seemed more vibrant and crunchy, and the cider tasted sweeter. Cynthia had been by his side for years, but now that she was truly *by his side*, the world was a better place. He had much to be thankful for.

She had met with her old therapist several times already after their difficult evening, and though she hadn't talked much about it, her therapy sessions seemed to be helping. Her peaceful and silly countenance was back, and there hadn't been any more "freak-outs," as she called them, even on the two occasions that they found themselves in a heated kiss on her living room couch.

Mitt and Connie had arrived a week ago and planned to stay for another few days, and they had the same reaction everyone else had to the announcement that Wyatt and Cynthia were a couple. If there was a scoreboard for reactions, the score would read *Not Surprised 100, Surprised 0.*

Well, actually two. He and Cynthia were the only ones surprised that they had fallen for each other years ago.

He skipped up the steps to her house and was warmly greeted by Mitt and Roscoe. Cynthia had asked Wyatt to drive her to Evelyn's early so that she could help with the food, and he was more than happy to oblige.

She greeted him with a kiss on the cheek. "You're right on time. The food is loaded in boxes on the table."

He and Mitt took them to the car while Cynthia got her coat on. When she got into the car, he leaned over to give her a proper kiss. "Happy Thanksgiving, lady I'm most thankful for."

"Happy Thanksgiving, man I'm most thankful for."

"I'm really thankful for the extra time with you this morning, even if it's only a few minutes. We haven't had much alone time since your parents got to town."

"I know. I've missed you." She got a mischievous grin on her face. "I may have exaggerated how early I promised to be at Evelyn's. Can we take a detour down to the lake?"

"Are you kidding? More time with you is a Thanksgiving miracle!"

Evelyn's B and B was close to Hideaway Beach, so it wasn't much of a detour. Lake Michigan was showing its deepest blue, and the sky had wisps of clouds that looked like an artist had put just the right number of brush strokes on it.

Cynthia cleared her throat. "So . . . I saw you and my parents huddled together last night . . . ."

"Who, us?" He gave her his most angelic smile.

"We need to talk before you get any big ideas about proposing."

He raised his hands in surrender. "Okay, I will agree to whatever your terms are."

"I'm serious."

"So am I. What do we need to talk about?"

"The bedroom."

He felt color fill his face and a slack jaw replace his teasing grin.

"I still don't know when I'll be ready for things to get physical, so you may want to hold off on that proposal."

He smiled proudly at her. "Look at you, saying no. And watch this—whatever you say, dear." The teasing grin was back. "I'm kidding, but I promised I wouldn't pressure you and you know I mean it. I told you, second base on our fifth anniversary, remember?"

She looked determined as she squeezed his hand. "I know you mean that, but I want us to have a real wedding night with all that entails, and I'm working on getting ready for it in therapy. I want every part of our marriage to be great, including that, but it's going to take work."

"Work, huh?" He winked at her. "Let me know if I can be of assistance."

She giggled. "Actually, you already have. Those recent make-out sessions? Those may have been homework assignments."

He threw his head back and laughed. "My lips have been your homework?"

"Yes, and the assignments have been very enjoyable."

"Very. I'm available for practice tests and pop quizzes too. Tutoring, the works. Anytime."

"How generous of you." She leaned over and kissed him tenderly.

He grinned at her when she pulled away. "Was that homework?"

"That was voluntary extra credit."

Chapter 33

CYNTHIA TURNED BACK TO watch the waves hit the shore, and they sat in comfortable silence for several minutes. "I know it's Thanksgiving and expected for us to say what we're thankful for, but I truly am thankful for you. Every day."

Wyatt took her hand and gave it a gentle squeeze. "I'm thankful for you too. More every day."

She looked at the time and groaned. "Now it really is time for me to get to Evelyn's to help."

"Okay, if we must." He leaned over and kissed her cheek. "I'm thankful for our bonus time here before we spend the rest of the day with a house full of people."

Since Evelyn's house was so close to the beach, they pulled into the back alley to park behind it in no time. Shelby waved them in through the back door. "Happy Thanksgiving! Auntie Ev is just pulling the pies out of the oven, and Clay is on his way out to help you unload the truck."

While the men unloaded the truck, Shelby and Cynthia snuck into the library to discuss Shelby's last dress fitting, scheduled for tomorrow. Shelby and Clay would be getting married in just under forty-eight hours, and excitement was oozing out of her, making her even more bubbly than usual.

"Cynthia, look what Aunt Evelyn found!" She handed her an elegant picture frame with her parents' wedding picture. "I can't believe what you did with my mom's dress. No one is going to believe it's the same one when I wear it down the aisle."

"She looks beautiful, but I'm glad you decided to get rid of those sleeves and change the neckline. I think the design we settled on is perfect for you."

"Me too. You did such a beautiful job on it." She carefully set the picture back on the desk. "I can't wait to wear it on my wedding day!"

Cynthia envied the happy bride, free to be excited about getting married. Shelby was not free of struggles though, Cynthia reminded herself. The health issues she had gone through over the past several years had made everything she did difficult and made her future full of uncertainty. As it was, her wedding date had largely been determined by a medication regimen.

She was getting aggressive treatments for Lyme disease and wanted to finish the harshest antibiotics before her wedding so she could feel less sick. The treatment protocol seemed to be working, and she was regaining strength every time Cynthia saw her. Shelby and Clay had no idea if infertility would be one of the effects of her disease or if she would ever be able to get back to the sports and activities they both loved, but they were plunging ahead with their life together. *She's trusting You and moving forward with it, Lord. Thank you for the reminder that we are not alone and that our futures are in Your hands—that You help us.*

Cynthia hugged Shelby. "I'm so happy for you and Clay. You two are a good example of walking by faith."

Just then they heard footsteps and looked up to see Clay leaning against the doorway. "Shelby, you promised . . . ."

She groaned teasingly. "Yes, dear." Stepping away from Cynthia, she stepped into his waiting arms. "I promised Clay that I would go lie down before everyone gets here so I don't get worn out. He's going to help you and Auntie Ev."

He kissed her on the cheek and gently pushed her toward the staircase before turning to Cynthia. "Okay, I'm all yours. What can I help with?"

"You really watch out for her."

"After all the begging I did to get her to marry me, I want to make sure she's able to enjoy the day. If she wears herself out, she'll be too sick to do that." He smiled as he looked back to watch her climb the stairs. "She promised that she'll do nothing tomorrow but the dress fitting and quick check of the decorations at the church when we're done, and I'm holding her to it."

Cynthia crossed her heart. "I promise I won't keep her a minute longer than I have to. The dress fit great the other day, so I'm sure it will be perfect tomorrow. She's going to be a beautiful bride."

Clay's grin grew. "She could wear her old running clothes and be a beautiful bride, but I know you'll make her look even more stunning than usual. Speaking of her dress, did you save all the material that you took out like I asked?"

"Of course. It's in a safe place and I'm praying that I get to use it for something for a baby someday."

He looked wistfully out the window. "I'm praying we get to use it for that too, but we'll see what God has for us. As long as my future has her in it, the rest is all icing on the cake."

Cynthia's heart swelled for the sweet couple. "I was just telling her that the two of you are a great example of walking in faith."

"Is there any other way?"

Indeed.

Chapter 34

WYATT ALMOST DROPPED THE box he was carrying when he walked into Evelyn's kitchen and saw Mitch in an apron.

Mitch didn't look up from the rolls he was carefully placing on a cookie sheet. "Not a word, Henry."

"You look pretty, Mitch." He wondered if he could grab his phone and take a picture as fast as Cynthia could. This was definitely a moment for posterity.

"Bella made me promise not to mess up my sweater before we get a picture in front of the mantle." He snickered in Wyatt's direction. "I'm still sure I look more manly than you did in the flowered sheet."

"You can't prove that was me. Where is Bella, anyway?"

"She's upstairs talking to her mother."

"Yikes, that sounds fun." From everything he had heard about Bella's family, it was no surprise that Bella had moved thousands of miles away from them.

"She wanted to get it over with before the party started so she can enjoy herself."

"Work before play. Smart woman." He moved closer to Mitch so he could lower his voice. "Are we set for the proposal?"

Mitch grinned. "I took the ring to Cynthia's yesterday so that I don't take the chance of forgetting it on the big night."

"Congratulations, man." He looked through the box and started unloading the potatoes he had just brought in.

"I told Cynthia we could have a double wedding, you know."

When Wyatt looked at him, he didn't see the smirk he expected. "I wish. She's not ready to think about dates or even letting me propose yet." *Lord, make it soon.*

Suddenly Mitch sobered as he wiped his hands on a towel and folded his arms across his chest. "I'm not surprised. She's been through a lot."

"She finally told me more about what she went through with Kirk. I'd like to break that guy in two for what he did to her."

"Get in line." The tension in Mitch's jaw showed Wyatt just how far he would go for his sister. "The night she left—I've never seen her look like that before or since. He was a scary dude that night. I've never faked toughness so much as that moment, but seeing the look on her face . . . Zack's . . . Let's just say I was ready to get them out of there by any means necessary." He shook his head, and Wyatt could see him fighting against clenching his fists.

"I'm glad you were there. Seeing the look on her face when she talked about it was enough for me. I wouldn't be me if I didn't tease her about getting married right away, but I'm not pushing anything with her. I'll wait forever if I have to."

Mitch nodded. "Did you talk to my parents?"

Wyatt smiled proudly. "I did, and their blessing is secured. All I need now is hers."

"You'll get it. Just give her time." He slapped Wyatt on the back and turned to pick up the cooler as Cynthia and Clay walked into the kitchen.

"Who's ready to peel some potatoes?"

Under Cynthia's direction, Wyatt and Clay started peeling while she and Evelyn organized the other groceries they had brought.

Mitch was filling the cooler and didn't notice Cynthia grabbing her phone and taking his picture until it was too late.

"Hey!"

That's my girl. "Don't bother trying to get that away from her, Mitch. She's probably already made it her home screen."

Cynthia giggled as she turned to Wyatt. "Nope, I'm not changing that anytime soon. You in a flowered skirt beats all other options."

Bella came in and walked straight over to Mitch, who pulled her into his arms.

"How's Mommy Dearest?"

"Just as warm and charming as ever. She says hello to everyone, by the way."

"Sure she does."

Bella chuckled and kissed him on the cheek. "She really did. She didn't mean it, but she said it. Manners, you know. Now that the call is over, I can enjoy my day with a real family." She delivered quick hugs to Wyatt and Cynthia before she stepped back and took in the sight of Mitch in the apron and grinned.

Cynthia spoke over her shoulder as she took over Mitch's duty with the rolls. "I just texted a picture of him to you, Bella. You're welcome."

"Okay, honey." Bella started pulling Mitch toward the kitchen door. "Let's go get our picture so you can get out of that ridiculous thing."

Mitch raised his arm in victory as he let her lead him out of the room.

Wyatt watched them walk out the door, then looked over at Clay, who was focusing on peeling the potatoes to perfection. By the end of the weekend, Clay would be married and Mitch would be engaged.

And he would be waiting.

Chapter 35

CYNTHIA AND EVELYN EXCHANGED a satisfied smile as they, along with the last of their helpers, left the kitchen to join the games being played in the parlor.

The rest of the guests had set up game tables, and the shouts of "Yahtzee!" and cries of defeat over other games filled the air, mixing with the ever-increasing aroma of the turkey. Laci had ridden with Garrett and Brianna, and the three of them were playing a quiet game of Euchre with Zachary. Brianna's parents, siblings, and siblings-in-law played Candyland with her niece at the table.

Cynthia watched Laci closely. She looked like she hadn't slept and was just going through the motions. Zachary had shared that he had asked her straight out what was going on in her relationship, and Laci had promptly shown him to the door and refused to take his calls or answer his texts for several days. At least they were back to talking. Sort of. Laci had been quieter with her too, when they worked on sewing projects, and Cynthia went along with it when Laci said she was just concentrating on the projects she was working on and trying not to mess up.

Cynthia sat at the table where the Candyland game was being played and watched as the adults cheated to make sure three-year-old Lily won. As her eyes scanned the room, she saw people she had known for years mingling with those who were new in town. She knew some of their stories and heartaches and was inspired by the faith they had all shown.

While they ate their dinner, everyone shared at least one thing they were thankful for. Some people thought the tradition was cliché, but Cynthia always appreciated some of the answers that people at this table came up with. There were thanks for finding lost relatives, surviving heart attacks and car accidents, for marriages and pregnancies, job changes, and renewed relationships with God.

Tears came to her eyes when Zachary again thanked everyone for praying for him when he was having such a hard time and talked about being thankful for decreased flashbacks and nightmares. Her heart leaped when she saw Laci reach over and squeeze his hand, and she sent up a silent prayer for healing in their friendship. When it came to Wyatt's turn, he said simply, "I'm thankful that I finally had my eyes opened to what was right under my nose."

Sitting at that table, she realized just how thankful she was and what a wonderful life she had. Her parents, her son, her love, her sister and her family, and her friends made her life overflow with goodness. Just like so many others at the table, she knew she could lean on God to carry her through the next phase of her life. Maybe, just maybe, she didn't have to put that off for long. With God's and Wyatt's help, she could take one day and step at a time toward her future.

Mitch, Bella, Zachary, and a few others took care of the dishes and insisted that everyone who was still at Evelyn's relax after dinner. Laci had quietly excused herself and left soon after eating, which drew a look between Garrett and Brianna. *They know too.* Cynthia prayed for Laci's protection and thanked God for giving her a concerned brother who was doing what he could to look out for her.

Mom and Dad, as well as Sarah and her family, had promised some old friends that they would go there for pie, so they had left right after dinner too. Several others had family obligations to get to as well, so the crowd was thinning out. Wyatt and Joe Callahan had offered to look at Evelyn's furnace to see what the strange noise she had noticed was and had been downstairs for some time.

Cynthia joined Evelyn and some of the other guests in the parlor and enjoyed a cup of tea with them. Sisters-in-law Emily Callahan and Claire Millard were exchanging pregnancy stories and comparing bellies on the other side of the room while they had their own tea party with Claire's husband, Quinn, and Emily's daughter, Lily, the reigning Candyland champion. Rick and Faith Weston talked excitedly with some B and B guests about the treatment center they had just created for pain and addiction on the edge of town. A few ladies from church were huddled in one corner discussing a needlepoint project one was working on. Cynthia and Evelyn sat together on the couch and stretched their feet out on the elegant coffee table, which felt rather scandalous.

"You really have the perfect home for a day like today, Evelyn. Thank you for continuing the tradition."

"This is one of my favorite days of the year. I'll always host the Thanksgiving Fellowship Meal." Evelyn leaned over and kept her voice low. "It seems everything has gotten back to smoother waters for you and Wyatt."

Cynthia leaned back and smiled. Evelyn was closer to her mother's age than her own, but she had always been the easiest person to talk to in Cynthia's life. She had been her confidant since she was a pregnant teenager and knew more than almost anyone about Cynthia's past and struggles. She was the only person other than Wyatt and her therapist that Cynthia had confided in about the night Zachary was conceived, and her words of comfort and encouragement had helped pull Cynthia out of a deep hole of shame. "It has. It's hard to believe that we fit together as well as we do. As corny as it sounds, it feels meant to be."

Evelyn chuckled and Cynthia playfully slapped her hand. "I know, I know, everyone saw it but us. We've still got some challenges ahead, but I know we're going to make it."

"I'm glad you decided to go back to therapy. You seem more relaxed."

Cynthia hid her giggle behind her tea cup. "She gave me homework to make out with Wyatt."

Evelyn laughed. "It sounds like therapy has changed since I tried it. I went once to see what all the fuss was about, and the therapist just stared at me and waited for me to talk. I like yours better."

"So does Wyatt. I'm afraid I might try his patience in that certain area. Is it pathetic to need a homework assignment from a shrink to make out with the man you love?"

Evelyn grasped Cynthia's hand. "Wyatt is an understanding man. Does he know everything?"

"Yes. I didn't give details, but he knows the basics. I owed him that."

"He knows what you've been through, and he's crazy about you. Of course, the rest of us have known you were meant to be together for years." She smiled as she picked up her tea and sipped it. That was the closest thing to sarcasm that would ever come out of Evelyn Glover.

"We're never going to live that down, are we?"

"It's just part of your story, dear. God was preparing you for each other and knew you needed time."

"I wouldn't want things any other way, then." God was not only preparing them for each other, He was preparing her to live as a married woman the way He intended. He would be part of every aspect of Wyatt and Cynthia's marriage, just as He was their Matchmaker.

Just then, Wyatt and Joe walked into the room and announced that the furnace was fixed. When Wyatt's eyes met hers, Cynthia's heart skipped a beat.

I'm going to marry that man.

Chapter 36

"A LITTLE TO THE left . . . wait, go back to the right . . . stop right there. Perfect."

Wyatt and Zack held the Christmas tree in front of the picture window while Mitch tightened the screws in the stand from his position on the floor. The fat Douglas Fir took up the whole window and a good portion of the room, but it was the one Cynthia had declared perfect at the tree farm.

Cynthia almost squealed with glee. "I love it! Hot chocolate now or after we decorate it?"

Wyatt and Zack looked at each other and made faces before answering in unison with Mitch. "Both!"

"Coming right up." She slipped into the kitchen with Connie and Bella close on her heels.

When they returned, Wyatt and Zack had watered it and gotten the old tree skirt arranged around the bottom under Mitt's expert direction. Cynthia's tray was full of mugs of hot cocoa with home-made marshmallows and Connie's was full of fresh cookies. Bella was behind them with small plates and napkins.

Cynthia's sister, Sarah, and her husband and two children, still in town for their Thanksgiving visit, walked through the door just as everyone was grabbing their favorite cookies from the tray. "We brought fresh donuts! And don't worry, Mitch. We got you an extra nutty one."

The sugar and decorating feast continued until the last ornament was on the tree. Zack had the honor of putting the angel on top, and everyone spontaneously cheered when she was in place. Wyatt loved being with Cynthia's family, and seeing the look of peace and happiness on her face when she was around the people she loved filled the deepest recesses of his heart.

After receiving the cue from Mitch, Cynthia lit candles around the room and changed the song on the Christmas playlist Wyatt had connected to the speaker earlier. She nodded at Wyatt, and he turned the lights off. The room was beautiful, lit only by candles, the fireplace, and Christmas lights.

Bella was looking at all the old family ornaments on the tree when she finally noticed that the loquacious family had gone uncharacteristically silent. When she turned around to find Mitch on one knee holding out the engagement ring he and Cynthia had both thought most suited her at the antique stores, she gasped. When she gave a tearful "yes," the family erupted in applause and noise again. Mitch had obviously made the right call when he decided to have the family be part of the proposal. Bella's snobby family had practically disowned her when she left her cheating husband and old life behind, and being welcomed by all of Mitch's family clearly touched her.

Wyatt wished a proposal could be so easy for himself and Cynthia. On the way home from Evelyn's on Thanksgiving he had promised her that despite his teasing, he wouldn't rush or pressure her about either their engagement or wedding date. He was going to have to read her carefully to know when she was ready for it, but he could wait. The ring that was hidden in the safe in his closet wasn't going anywhere, and neither was she.

He gazed across the room at Cynthia, who was hugging the newly-engaged couple. *I'll wait forever for that precious gem if I have to.*

She looked over at him and met his smile. Her gaze never left his as she made her way across the living room to him. Clasping his hands in hers, she leaned up and kissed him.

"More extra credit?"

"Mmm-hmm."

After the rest of the family left, Cynthia led him over to the Christmas tree and they stood arm in arm looking at it. He could stand there all night with the soft glow and her at his side. He almost forgot that Zack was sitting in the chair on the other side of the tree. Suddenly it was Cynthia who was down on one knee grinning at him.

What is she doing?

She took his hand in hers. "Wyatt Henry, I've loved you for far longer than I realized. Will you please make me the happiest woman around and propose to me whenever you see fit?"

Yes! He met her there on the floor and pulled her into his arms. "You bet your life I will—when you least expect it, of course."

Zack clapped and cheered yet again, then walked over and hugged the two of them together. "Mommy! Daddy!"

Wyatt laughed, but he knew there was a serious note in Zack's joke. He turned and hugged him tightly. "I couldn't ask for a better son."

Chapter 37

CYNTHIA AND WYATT SAT sipping their coffee together in front of the Christmas tree a week later. It was always her favorite time of the year, and she felt like the picture of contentment.

"I'm really enjoying having you come over for morning coffee before work. I could definitely get used to this."

"And someday I won't even have to cross the street or put on shoes to have coffee in this living room with you." He raised his mug. "Here's to that day."

She raised her mug to meet his. "That will be a great day."

"How is the sewing apprenticeship going with Laci?"

"It's good. She's such a huge help, and we're almost caught up with my order pile. She has a natural talent."

"Has she opened up much yet?"

"Not a lot, so I just keep waiting and praying." Cynthia longed for the day she could give a different answer. "She's been on my mind even more than usual today. I spent some time praying for her strength and courage before you got here."

"Is she still keeping Zack at arm's length?" It was comforting to see that Wyatt cared as much as she did about the situation.

She nodded. "Pretty much. I warned him that she might do that if he asked her outright if something was going on and demanded answers from her. I wish he would have listened to me."

"I'll bet he does too. He was so worked up about you that day that I don't think a team of wild horses could have stopped him. His only focus was on helping her to get out so that she could avoid what you've gone through." He let out a heavy sigh. "What you still go through."

"I know." She picked at one of the pumpkin walnut muffins she'd made earlier in the morning. "I keep reminding him that she's responding the way a lot of victims do and to be patient and pray for her. He's still reaching out to her and inviting her to do things, but even though they're talking again, she keeps him at bay and only helps me on nights he's closing the store late. I can tell she misses him, so I think she'll come around eventually."

Wyatt seemed contemplative as he sipped his coffee. "I was glad to see him finally have a conversation with her brother on Thanksgiving."

"Me too. I think it helped him when Garrett told him straight out that he and Brianna have the same suspicions. Brianna has worked with women who have been victims of domestic violence, so I think she's giving him some guidance." If only Laci realized the support she had surrounding her.

"Good." He studied her with concern in his eyes. "How has this been for you lately?"

She reassured him with a smile. "Oddly enough, it's healing. Every time I pray for her and talk to her, I feel like I'm getting stronger too. And I just have a feeling that she's going to get out of that relationship."

Their talk was interrupted by a ding from her cell phone. She had stopped silencing it when Zachary left for war, and it had become habit to look at it if either he or Wyatt were away from home. When she glanced at the text message, she was glad she did.

"Well, how about that? It's from Laci." She read the message. "She's asking for prayer. She said she was inspired by my courage and she's breaking up with her boyfriend. Oh, thank You, Lord."

Wyatt let out a slow breath. "You know what this means though."

She nodded. "Now it gets more dangerous. I'm going to remind her not to be alone with him." Cynthia knew all too well how dangerous it was for a woman to break up with an abusive man who hadn't decided he was done with her yet. She typed a quick note of caution and prayed for her courage and safety as she hit *Send*.

Wyatt gestured toward the phone. "Ask her if she wants me to go with her. I'll go as a friend but one who happens to be in a police uniform."

Cynthia sent the offer to Laci. Laci responded quickly and declined, to Cynthia's great disappointment.

"She doesn't think that will be necessary, but she said to thank you." She hesitantly set her phone next to her. "This is the one time I don't like her natural optimism."

Wyatt picked up his phone and called the station to direct a squad car to patrol the area and be on alert.

"Thank you."

He smiled and tipped his imaginary hat. "Just part of keeping the community safe. That guy has had some run-ins with the cops in this area a couple of times, so it's not a problem to have eyes on him."

She picked her phone back up. "You know we have to tell Zachary. As much as I don't want him to worry or put himself at risk the way Mitch did for us, he'll never forgive me if I don't tell him."

Dialing the hardware store instead of Zachary's cell phone, she prayed that Mitch would answer. Thankfully, God answered that prayer.

"Can you talk?"

"I'm pretty sure we have that. Let me check in the back." They had developed code language when Zachary was going through his troubles, and it came in handy still.

She heard the click of Mitch's office door. "What's up, sis? Are you okay?"

"I have some news for Zachary that I don't want to tell him over the phone. I was hoping you would break it to him."

"Uh-oh, what's going on?"

"Laci texted me and said she's planning to break up with her boyfriend. You know how bad that can be." Beyond his experience with Cynthia, Mitch had also witnessed Bella's ex-husband become aggressive when she stood up to him, so he was familiar with the potential danger.

"He's been acting antsy and looking at his phone non-stop for the past ten minutes, so I think she may have already told him."

"Okay, I suppose that's good. You can let him know that Wyatt has put out the word with the police department, and they will do some patrols in her neighborhood and be on the lookout. It helps that her boyfriend is not a stranger to them."

"Yes, it does. I'll talk to him and let you know if I hear anything."

Concentrating was practically impossible through the rest of the day, so Cynthia finally gave up and spent her time talking to God about Laci and about her own history.

Her healing was coming along nicely, and she was feeling more comfortable with the idea of sharing a home and a life with Wyatt. She was even finding herself getting impatient now that she had given him permission to propose and he hadn't given a hint about doing so. Chuckling at the irony that he was now the one taking his sweet time, she started sketching her wedding dress.

It had been years since she had allowed herself to think about a wedding of her own, but she found that the dreams she had about a beautiful dress were alive and well. She had learned a lot about making dresses match the bride's personality, and it was fun to use her skills in preparation for her own special day. The dress was the only tradition that she really cared about. Now that she finally had her groom, that was all that mattered.

Chapter 38

WYATT TOOK THE LONG way home and drove through Laci's neigh-borhood as well as her soon-to-be-ex boyfriend's. Seeing no sign of trouble, he said a prayer and kept going.

Cynthia was waiting with a mug of hot cocoa when he got to her house. As she set down the cup and greeted him with a hug, she started laughing. "I just almost welcomed you home. I guess I'm getting ahead of myself."

"Good, I was hoping you would be practicing that line." He gave her a kiss on the cheek and a tight squeeze that he hoped made her feel desired but not possessed. She offered her lips for a more intimate kiss, which he obliged. "I love helping you with your homework."

She winked as she stepped out of his arms. "That hasn't been my homework for two weeks. That was all me."

"Even better. It's nice to know that you want to kiss me even when you're not getting credit for it. Have you heard anything from Laci?"

She frowned and her brow furrowed with concern. "Not yet."

Zack walked through the back door with his phone in his hand, looking relieved. "I just heard from Laci. She said everything went okay, but she sounds pretty down. Would you mind if I invited her to come over for dinner?"

Cynthia smiled. "Of course not. Especially since it's your turn to cook."

He started swiping and tapping on his phone screen. "It's my turn to provide dinner, not necessarily cook. I'm ordering pizza."

When Laci arrived at the house, she looked shaken but in one piece. Since Zack had just left to pick up the pizza, Wyatt made up an excuse to go across the street for a few minutes to give the ladies time to talk. When he saw Zack return, he walked back over. Laci and Cynthia were in the kitchen putting molasses cookie dough balls on a baking sheet and talking about Christmas carols. Cynthia gave him a subtle nod that told him everything was okay.

During dinner Laci told them that she had taken Cynthia's advice and broken up with Ronnie over the phone in case he went into a rage. From her description, he was angry but the conversation went more smoothly than Wyatt and Cynthia had feared it might. When she said that he had driven by her house a couple of times but there happened to be a police car on the street both times, Cynthia and Wyatt shared a look.

Laci looked back and forth between them before landing on him. "Wait a minute, did you have something to do with that?"

He hoped she wouldn't be upset, but wasn't going to lie. "I may or may not have asked some people to swarm your neighborhood today, just as a precaution."

She looked down and played with her half-eaten pizza for a moment. Her eyes were misty when she met his. "Thank you, Wyatt. He was really mad, and you probably prevented something today."

He tried to hide his surprise as he nodded in response. It was the closest she had come to sharing anything about the potential abuse in the relationship with any of them. *Progress.*

When Cynthia and Zack started taking the plates to the kitchen, Wyatt reached into his pocket and pulled out the card with the domestic violence hotline number on it and handed it to her. "Just in case this would be helpful. You also have my number, and I want you to call or text me if you need help at any time."

Chapter 39

FINALLY! CYNTHIA LOOKED AT what used to be the big pile of alteration orders. "We did it, Laci."

Laci grinned. "This is awesome, but I'm kind of bummed out that we're done. This has been really fun."

"You say that as if we're finished."

Laci looked at the empty chair that was once piled high. "I thought we were."

"We're done with that pile and with Ainsley Baldwin's wedding dress and veil, but I've got three people coming today and two tomorrow with dresses they want altered or remade for holiday parties."

Laci bounced in her seat. "Yes! I love party dresses!"

"And in the meantime . . ." Cynthia pulled over the basket of fabric scraps and set it between herself and Laci. "Let's have a lesson so we can get to working on your stuff."

"Oh, yay! I thought you forgot, and I didn't want to bug you about it."

"Heck no. We had a deal." She nudged the basket closer to her. "Pick out any fabric you like from here."

As Laci started looking through the scraps, she paused and met Cynthia's gaze. "Thank you for everything you've done. I know I haven't said much about Ronnie, but I've heard every word you've said."

Cynthia's breath caught. *Thank You, Lord.* "That's been my prayer for you. You don't deserve to be hurt, Laci. You deserve to be with someone who treats you well and appreciates you."

Laci looked down. "Well, I'm not sure about that, but I know that I would rather be alone than with Ronnie."

"That's a good start. Give yourself some time." Cynthia reached out and grasped her hand. "You know, your mother would be very proud of you for walking away from that."

Chapter 40

WYATT WAS ALMOST FINISHED shoveling his sidewalk. He had done Cynthia's first and tried to make enough noise that she would notice and fire up some hot cocoa for him. Despite the layers of clothing, he was starting to freeze. He had forgotten to put on the scarf that Cynthia had made for him a few years back, and his neck was surely getting frostbitten.

As he shoveled, he prayed. *Lord, she seems ready for a proposal. Is she ready?*

He was pushing the snow from the step when something cold and hard hit his unprotected neck. The giggles were his first clue about the source of the attack.

When he turned to see Cynthia standing in his driveway laughing, he was struck by the joy on her face. *What did I ever do to deserve such a magnificent creature?*

He slowly bent down to grab a big handful of snow without breaking eye contact with her. She stared him down while reloading her own hands and forming her weapons.

Walking slowly and carefully watching her for any indications that she was about to throw the next one, he made his way to where she was standing. He tried to make his eyes look sultry to distract her, even though he had no idea how to do that or what it even meant.

When he got close enough, he grabbed her and pulled her into an embrace. Just when he was about to stick his snowball down the back of her coat, she beat him to it, shoving hers up the back of his.

When he flinched, he lost his balance and fell into the pile of snow left by the plow a few hours ago, taking her with him. He had never been one to waste an opportunity, so he pulled her into a kiss. Her giggle broke it off, which was just as well. The snow was seeping into every spot he'd left uncovered, and he was freezing.

She was still laying on top of him when she stopped laughing long enough to speak. "I just came out to tell you that your hot cocoa is ready."

"Well, you have a heck of a way of announcing that!"

She gave him a quick peck on the lips again and shrugged as she started to get up. "I'm trying to keep things interesting."

The snow collapsed underneath her and she fell deeper into it, making her laugh harder. They both sat up and used each other as leverage to stand together.

"Come on, your hot chocolate is getting cold." She reached out her hand to take his as he looked up to see Zack and Laci walking to Laci's car and laughing at them.

When they got closer, Zack turned to Laci and snickered. "I hope you're not expecting those two to grow up any time soon."

"Why would we want to do that?" Wyatt turned to Cynthia and shook his head. "Kids these days."

It felt great to walk into the warm house, and he was glad to see the fire roaring. His jeans were wet all the way through, and he was shivering.

She took one look at them and started toward the linen closet. "Those need to go in the dryer. I'll get your pretty flowered sheet."

"Do you have one in a more manly pattern?"

She winked as she tossed the same flowered one to him. "Of course I do."

They met back in the kitchen a minute later, he in his flowered sheet and she in a new pair of flannel pajama bottoms that were actually her size. He put their clothes into the dryer while she ladled the hot cocoa into mugs.

When they sat on the couch in the living room, they snuggled together as closely as they could and piled blankets across their laps.

He looked down at her pink, smiling face. "Your lips look like they could use some warming up. It just so happens that lip-warming is a complementary part of my snow-shoveling services."

"I don't know. They're pretty cold. It might take a while."

"I've got all evening." *And the rest of my life.*

Chapter 41

CYNTHIA SAT MESMERIZED IN First Community Church. Christmas Eve services were always her favorite, and this was even better than the others. The warm glow of the candles as they sang *Silent Night* filled the tiny sanctuary, and she felt as if her heart and life were more full than they had ever been. She hadn't realized during all the years that she had spent guarding herself from the bad that she limited the good that could come in too.

Standing between the two men she most treasured, she anticipated the future with a new fervor and felt ready for anything that would come her way. She studied the stained-glass windows and thought of the families that had gone there together through the years. Several of the people she knew there had been going to First Community Church for their whole lives, as had the generations before them. Having visited there for services and weddings over the years, she was always struck by the history in the old sanctuary.

She pictured a day in the future when a daughter-in-law and grandchildren would complete their row. As usual it was Laci's face she pictured, but it was God's role to choose a wife for her son, not hers. He had done better than she could when He brought

Wyatt into her life, and she trusted that He would provide the right person for Zachary too.

When the lights came up and they blew the candles out, Cynthia pulled her two men into a hug. "This is the best Christmas Eve of my life."

Zachary's attention was quickly taken by Laci, who had recently switched to First Community along with her brother. Brianna's family was one of those that had attended for generations, and Garrett and Laci had joined them for the service.

"Mom, I know it's Christmas Eve, but are you going to be okay with me going over to the Callahans' with Laci for a while? Brianna invited us both, and Laci asked me to go."

"Of course, honey. Despite her smiles, she looks like she needs you tonight."

Cynthia prayed for the sweet girl who had been through so much in the previous months, between losing her father and breaking free from her boyfriend. She knew God would mend Laci's heart just as He had hers and was glad that she had let Zachary back in. That friendship was good for both of them.

She felt Wyatt's face near her ear as they slowly made their way from the pew to the crowded aisle, hugging people and offering Christmas greetings as they went. "At the risk of sounding unsociable, let's go home."

There was no one she wanted to be with more than Wyatt for what was left of Christmas Eve, so she maneuvered through the crowd quickly and led him out into the crisp air. They strolled slowly down the quiet street to his truck, her hand firmly tucked in his and her ears tuned to the snow crunching under their feet.

As if the snowy scene demanded reverence, he spoke quietly. "Since Zack decided to go with Laci, can I give you some of my gifts tonight? They're personal."

"You can give me personal gifts any time you want."

When they got home, Wyatt took Roscoe with him when he went to his house to retrieve his gifts so he could give him a quick walk. Cynthia lit candles and the Christmas tree and put on her favorite Christmas hymn playlist after starting the hot chocolate warming. She skipped the lamps, preferring the cozy glow she had just created that would get brighter as soon as Wyatt got back and started a fire. It was the perfect ambiance for Christmas Eve.

When Wyatt walked in and looked around, he had a look of childlike wonder on his face. "Wow, this is what every night should look like. This room is almost as beautiful as you are."

"Aww, you sure know how to make a girl's night." She took his coat and hung it on his usual hook.

"I didn't want to make you feel self-conscious by saying anything earlier, but that dress is amazing." She had seen him noticing it—noticing her—earlier, and instead of the familiar tension, it had sent a warm shiver through her.

She looked down and admired it herself. "Thank you. I just finished it yesterday, and it's one of my favorites."

"It's one of my favorites too. I haven't been able to take my eyes off you all night."

She felt the heat rise in her cheeks as she leaned up and kissed him on the cheek. "Good."

It was a new experience to feel beautiful and to be comfortable with him noticing. After all the years of hiding in her clothes and trying to avoid the attention of men, it was nice to have it from the right one, the one who fell in love with her even when she dressed in personal armor.

She went to the kitchen to finish the hot cocoa and put some Christmas cookies on a plate while he started the fire. The crackling of the wood when she returned only added to the ambiance.

He pulled a gift bag out from behind his back and grinned at her.

She couldn't imagine what he couldn't wait until Christmas Day to give to her. "Before I accept any gifts tonight, this doesn't mean that you won't be coming over in your pajamas tomorrow morning, does it?"

"Of course not! Tradition is tradition."

"Maybe next year you'll be waking up here on Christmas Day." She was surprised at the increasing ease with which she thought and talked about the future when they would be married and live under the same roof.

"I certainly hope so." He led her over to the couch and sat next to her with the bag on his other side.

She leaned around him to look at the bag. "Hey, isn't that supposed to be my special gift?"

"Yes, but there's an order to them."

"Ooh, *them?*"

"Them."

She was intrigued as he pulled a small box that had a simple organza bow tied around it out of the bag. The exquisite carved wood box looked like it had come from one of the antique stores she had scoured with Mitch when he was deciding on the perfect engagement ring a few weeks ago.

When she opened it, she saw a delicate silver filigree heart locket. "Oh, it's so beautiful!"

As he took it and clasped it around her neck, he smiled down at her. "This is to remind you always that you have my undying love."

"Oh, honey, that's so sweet. I love it."

The second box was a little larger than the first, and she could hear something rattling around in it as she tore off the wrapping paper. Inside were what looked like Scrabble pieces that had been painted with a *yes* on one side and a *no* on the other. She looked at them in confusion.

"These are dual-purpose. First, they are my promise that my yes will always be yes and my no will always be no. I'll always be honest with you and I'll always do what I say." She fingered the tiny squares as he continued. "Second, and more importantly, I will always treasure your yes and respect your no. I will never pressure or push you for anything. And that includes a wedding date."

With every word he said, she wanted that wedding date closer. She leaned up and kissed him. "These are the most amazing things I've ever gotten."

"There's one more."

She was conflicted. Part of her wanted it to be a ring and proposal, but she had always hated the idea of having special events or anniversaries on holidays and had never been shy about sharing her opinion. Now she wished she had kept her big mouth shut.

He pulled out the last gift, a bigger and significantly heavier box. The gold embossed wrapping paper was so elegant and beautiful that she opened it slowly and carefully, not wanting to rip it. A thrill went through her when she opened it to see a Bible inscribed with *Cynthia Henry* on the cover. She followed the letters with her finger.

"I know it's a little early for your name change, but this is to remind you that when I finally get to be your husband, I will follow this book as my guide and will love you as Christ loves the church—sacrificially and eternally."

Tears streamed down her face before she noticed they'd started. "I love every one of my gifts. I love the giver even more. Thank you." She showed her appreciation with a kiss before snuggling into his arms. "My gifts are perfect."

He wiped her tears away with his thumb and gave her a teasing smile. "Are you disappointed that I didn't propose?"

"A little, but I've always told you I didn't like holiday proposals, so I didn't expect one. I couldn't love my gifts or you more."

"That's good." The curve of his lips and twinkle in his eyes told her he was up to something.

He was fidgeting with something in his right hand, and whatever it was sparkled in the candle light.

Could it be? She felt like a child who couldn't resist peeking to see if the thing they wanted most was under the Christmas tree.

"Wyatt, what do you have there?" She tried angling around him to see it.

"Nothing, just a rock. It's nothing." The smirk on his face told her everything.

"Wyatt Henry, are you playing with my ring? That's mine and I want it." She tried reaching out and grabbing his hand, but he held it just out of her reach, laughing the whole time.

"What would you want with this silly thing? You hate Christmas proposals."

"Not anymore!" She threw her arm out, making a valiant attempt to grab it. "Let me see it. Please?"

Suddenly he stopped and pulled her close, still keeping his hand out of reach. His breath was growing heavy, but his eyes had a glint she hadn't seen before as he grinned at her. "I told you it would be when you least expected it. Tonight is the one night I knew you wouldn't expect it."

Her hands flew to her face. She was suddenly overwhelmed with a feeling of being truly loved and of loving the man in front of her with every fiber of her being. When he slid down to one knee, her eyes turned into waterfalls.

He seemed as overcome with emotion as she was, and he had to take a couple of deep breaths and clear his throat before speaking. "Cynthia, will you be an old married couple who live in the same house with me?"

She couldn't force the word out. This was too much, too wonderful, too perfect.

She reached into the box with the cubes, fumbling for her answer. Holding it up, she showed him the *yes* that had been years in the making and that she had been afraid she would never have.

Her hand was shaking when she held it out to receive the ring. This time the shaking was all excitement.

She wound her fingers around his neck and pulled him near, impatient for his lips to meet hers. No one had to tell her to enjoy his kiss, and no one had to remind her that he was good and safe and only wanted to love her.

When he sat back next to her, they both stared at the ring as it shone in the candlelight. "I love it, Wyatt. It's perfect."

"I love you."

She turned to look at him and found him looking down at her with tears glistening in his eyes. When he pulled her close, she felt like she was made for that spot, for him. When he kissed her again, she felt the room spin.

This time when he tightened his hold on her, she did the same. The fear wasn't completely gone, but she knew there was no safer place than his arms.

She would stay there forever.

Now that Laci has finally walked away from that rotten abusive boyfriend, is there a chance for her and Zack? Keep reading for a peek of their story!

A Note From the Author

Ahh, Wyatt and Cynthia . . . once again, characters who were supposed to have tiny little roles expanded and needed a book of their own. When I first introduced Cynthia in Repairing Hearts, she was only supposed to have a small part in Mitch's story. I loved the close relationship she had with both Mitch and Zack, and I loved the strength we saw in her—especially because she had been abused in the past. As that story progressed, a tiny little thought about giving her a story someday formed way in the back of my mind. But when Mitch was on his way to her house when Zack was in crisis, Wyatt Henry was born. I don't even remember thinking about bringing in another character at that point. He just showed up. That's so like him to show up when he's needed, right? As soon as the idea of a cop friend popped into my mind, I knew that he lived across the street from Cynthia, that they were best friends, and that they were completely clueless that they were meant for each other.

When it came time to tell their story, all I knew about them apart from what we learned in Repairing Hearts was that she was a seamstress and that they both had reasons for not pursuing romantic relationships. There had to be a good reason they wouldn't be together. Sometimes those friends-to-love stories can have a pretty thin premise, so I wanted a solid reason that neither of them had pursued anything or pined away for the other. Her reason was a no-brainer because of her past, and his made sense to me because of his sacrificial and protective nature. I liked the idea that he wanted to be with her but had intentionally locked that desire away to protect her.

I had so much fun writing this story, and I wrote it faster than any of my other books. Their banter kept drawing me back to the manuscript, and after what she went through in her previous relationship, I loved giving her a protective man who treasured her, made her feel safe, and made her laugh. One of the most fun things when writing this was showing how they operated as a well-oiled machine. I'm telling you, I could have written ten books with them playing off each other. It also helped that I had a foot injury and was stuck soaking it in Epsom salt for a week. That and the story kept me glued to my chair!

This is the book that I've gotten the most emails about, and I've heard from women from all over who have either been in an abusive relationship or had sisters, friends, etc. who have. Hearing them say that the story rang true and that it gave them hope that someone could have a healthy relationship after being abused brought tears to my eyes every single time. That, my friend, is God at work. I thought I was just telling a story about a woman with a painful past and the man who was perfect for her. God always knows better. If you or someone you know is experiencing abuse (even if you aren't sure), please reach out to a local hotline or (for US residents) the National Domestic Violence Hotline at 800-799-7233 or text START to 88788.

Wyatt and Cynthia have big parts in Zack and Laci's story, so we haven't seen the last of them. Spoiler alert: Zack and Laci will beat Wyatt and Cynthia to the altar—on page one of their book! How did that happen?

If this is the first Summit County book you've read, you can learn more about some of the side characters in previous books. Zack,

Cynthia, and Wyatt were all introduced in Mitch and Bella's story, Repairing Hearts (Book 5), which took place during Zack's struggles. Laci was introduced in Garrett and Brianna's story, Returning Home (Book 6), and Garrett's suspicions about what was going on in her relationship were right on. If you guessed that the rest of the crowd on Thanksgiving have been in previous books, you're right—I'm not even going to put into words how happy it made me to talk about Clay and Shelby's wedding or Emily and Claire's pregnancies!

If you want to be the first to see a sneak peek of new books and hear about sales as well as see pictures from the real place that looks like Summit County, please subscribe to my newsletter by following the instructions for the QR code on the last page of the book! Newsletters aren't for everyone, so if you would just like to be notified of new releases, you can follow me on Amazon or Bookbub and they'll email you.

Thank you for spending your valuable time with my imaginary friends. If you would like to leave a one or two sentence review on Amazon or Bookbub so that other readers can be introduced to this book, I would be so grateful! They are one of the best ways for readers to find new to-them authors and books. If leaving a review is just too much (I get it ~ they take precious time that could be spent reading!), but you'd like to leave a rating instead, you can do that too! Thanks for reading!

See you in Summit County,

Katherine

Playing Married in Summit County

Can two best friends convincingly fake a whirlwind courtship and marriage long enough to find a home for a baby in need of protection?

Zack Huntley and Laci Ryan have been best friends since first grade. They've been there for each other through thick and thin, most recently through his war injuries and her exit from an abusive relationship. Neither has ever been willing to risk what they have by declaring their feelings for the other, so the friendship has remained just that.

Even after adjusting to life with his prosthetic leg and being treated for PTSD, Zack has declared himself unfit for relationships. He lost his chance with the only girl he ever loved because of his own cowardice, so his post-Army life will be focused on college classes and creating a new business, not the things he can't have.

Laci's normal joy is returning after finally getting away from the man who spent two years beating her down mentally and physically. After going against her own convictions and morals, she's certain that no good man—or even God—will want her, but she's determined to build a new life from the rubble.

When a positive pregnancy test leads to more threats, Laci needs someone to sign on the dotted line so that her baby can be adopted by safe and loving family. Best buddy Zack has always helped her, and this time is no different. They can hide a pregnancy and fake a marriage long enough to carry out their plan, right?

Sneak Peek ~ Playing Married in Summit County

Chapter 1

Zack Huntley tried to stand still in front of the Christmas tree, but his nerves were winning the battle inside him. Time seemed to stop as he waited for his bride to appear.

He straightened his tie and adjusted the sleeve of his suit again. Mitch, his uncle and best man, snickered and nudged him. "Dude, I know you're excited, but stop squirming." Their seven-year age difference, coupled with the fact that they spent most of their growing years under the same roof, made the thirty-year-old Mitch more like Zack's big brother than his uncle.

"Shut it, Mitch."

At least his nervousness looked like excitement. He straightened his shoulders as he had done for barracks inspections a thousand times and took a deep breath, focusing on the scent of pine and cinnamon in the air instead of his own nerves.

Mitch whispered in his ear. "Don't you have something in between hyper five-year-old and recruit at attention?"

He shot a fake glare in Mitch's direction. "Leave me alone. I'm nervous."

Mitch met his not-quite-glare with another snicker. "That's what you get for planning a wedding in five days."

"Remember this in a few months when you're the groom."

He took another deep breath and tried to relax. If he had known how nerve-racking it would be to stand there waiting for Laci to walk down the stairs, he would have pushed for a courthouse wedding, or at least an even smaller ceremony in Mom's living room. As it was, they were in Evelyn Glover's elegant Victorian parlor. Evelyn was a close friend of the family and honorary grandmother to Zack, and her home easily accommodated the crowd of twenty.

The ceremony should have been at the church. They were going to need all the help God was willing to give them, and if getting married in His house would give them a leg up, Zack was all for it. Unfortunately, his frazzled bride insisted they do it anywhere *but* a church, and he had acquiesced, asking God to bless and help them anyway.

Before his thoughts could go down the path of the challenges that lay ahead, the bridal processional music started. His breath caught in his throat when Laci appeared at the top of the stairs on the arm of her older brother, Garrett. Standing there in the pale blue evening gown that matched her eyes, she looked even more like an angel than usual. She looked different with most of her blonde curls tucked into an elegant updo, but she was as beautiful as ever.

They had been best friends since first grade when their teacher sat them together, and they had been there for each other through every major life event. From the normal childhood milestones of losing baby teeth and getting driver's licenses to the more devastating losses of her mother and his leg, they were there, side by side. Their bond was impenetrable, and no distance, relationship, or life event could weaken it. They fit together.

Still, he was as surprised as everyone else in the room that he was standing there moments away from becoming her husband.

She looked as nervous as he was. Even from where Zack was standing, he could see the death grip she had on Garrett's arm as they gradually made their way down the grand staircase. Maybe the old stairs weren't the wisest way for her to make an entrance, but they had thrown the wedding together so quickly that there hadn't been much time for deliberating over details.

Between her bouquet and the alterations she had made to her dress, the baby bump she was so nervous about was invisible to the naked eye. The only thing those gathered could see was the beautiful woman walking down the stairs, about to become his wife.

When she finally looked at him and smiled shyly, he let go of the breath he hadn't realized he had trapped in his chest. The tension on her face let up a bit when he smiled at her, and he willed her to keep taking steps and make the rest of the walk to his side.

As they approached, Garrett gave Zack the nod meant to convey his approval of the union. He had given it a couple of days ago when Zack had asked for his blessing, and Zack hoped he would still approve if he knew the truth.

Once next to Zack, Laci transferred her death grip from Garrett's arm to his. No wonder Garrett was grimacing. The strength that made the two of them competitive in everything from driveway basketball and beach volleyball to cornhole over the years was now choking off the blood supply to his arm.

He tried to listen to Pastor Ray's words as they stood there, but the moment she reached his side, his thoughts had become consumed by one thing—the kiss. It was coming—the very public, very awkward kiss that they hadn't discussed when they planned the wedding.

The kiss that he had wished for since he learned about kissing was about to happen, and in front of spectators, no less. Sweat broke out on the back of his neck.

Chapter 2

Laci Ryan held on to Zack's arm as if her life—or at the very least, her ability to stay upright—depended on it. She stretched up to whisper in his ear. "Are you sure about this?"

"Yes. Stop asking me that."

She tried to focus on Pastor Ray's words, but hearing about God's holy design for marriage sent a hot wave of shame through her. Shaking, she leaned into Zack and gripped his arm even harder.

He looked down at her and smiled, then reached over and loosened her fingers on his arm before covering them with his. "It's okay. I've got you."

As usual, she was comforted by his strength. She was so focused on using his arm to keep herself steady that he had to pull her hand from it when Pastor Ray asked them to turn toward each other to recite their vows. Handing her bouquet to Brianna Callahan, Garrett's girlfriend and her maid of honor, she took refuge in Zack's gentle brown eyes and the strong hands holding hers. They were doing this.

Suddenly she realized what was coming. The kiss! They hadn't talked about how they were going to handle that part. After years of wondering what it would be like to kiss him, she was about to find out. *Whatever you do, don't pass out.* She tried one of the breathing exercises he had taught her, but when she imagined his lips on hers, her lungs forgot how to work.

From the time she was a young girl, she had wanted to save her first kiss for her husband and had vowed to God that she would save it for her wedding. The irony that this would not be her first kiss, but it would be the first with her husband-to-be hit her like a hard slap to the face.

Print and ebook available on Amazon!

Acknowledgments

This book was startlingly easy to write, and I'm thankful that God used an injury to give me uninterrupted time in the writing chair. I've let Him know that in the future I'm happy to stay in my seat until the story is finished—no injury needed!

When I read (or in this case, write) stories with characters who have experienced the kind of pain and struggle in this book, I'm especially grateful for my own family. None of us are perfect, but family is supposed to be about being there for each other in good times and hard times. I don't know what I would do without the family I have.

The same can be said about friends. I don't want to brag, but I have some of the most amazing friends on this planet—including several I've met through the writing, editing, producing, and marketing of these stories. If I tried to name them individually, it would take another whole book.

It takes a village to put a book out, and my village of beta readers, editors, critique partner, proofreaders, and cover designer are beyond amazing. If you're reading this version of this note, you're seeing the new cover for this book (and series). My cover designer is so amazing that when I went out to take new pictures for this cover, he was texting back and forth with me about angles and shots. He deserves a special shout-out for this one!

Every time I see a review, social media post, or email from a reader who enjoys my books, I get a surge of gratitude. It takes time to tell me or others that you like the books, and I can't thank you enough. You are a true gift.

About the Author

Katherine Karrol is both a fan and an author of sweet Christian romance stories. Because she does not possess the ability or desire to put a good book down and generally reads them in one sitting, she writes books that can be read in the same way.

Her books are meant to entertain, encourage, and possibly inspire the reader to take chances, trust God, and laugh in the midst of this thing we call life. The people she interacts with in her professional world have absolutely no idea that she writes these books, so by reading this, you agree to keep her secret.

If you would like to talk about your favorite character, share who you were picturing as you were reading, or just chat about books and pretty places, you can email her at KatherineKarrol@gmail.com or follow her on the usual social media outlets. She's most active on Facebook, where she has a small reader group and loves to talk about books. The next most likely place to see evidence of her existence is Pinterest, where she has boards for all of her books, memes, and other bookish things. She seems to think that Instagram is a place to look at other posts but usually forgets to make her own. Maybe someday she'll get on the ball with that. Maybe.

Books

Summit County Series

Second Chance in Summit County

Trusting Again in Summit County

New Beginnings in Summit County

Taking Risk in Summit County

Repairing Hearts in Summit County

Returning Home in Summit County

Love Remembered in Summit County

Surprise Love in Summit County

Playing Married in Summit County

Hearts of Summit Series

Stay for Love

Open the camera app on your phone and aim it here to get a link to join my email community!

If the QR code is too confusing, just email me for the link :)

Made in United States
Orlando, FL
14 August 2022

21022651R00107